Abby's between girlfriends

A Sharing of Marital Secrets

To Dona
May God bless you!
Abby Gail Smith
8/11/01

A Sharing of Marital Secrets

By

Abby Gail Smith

Black Pearl Publishing, Dallas, Texas

Published by Black Pearl Publishing
P.O. Box 222088, Dallas, Texas 75222

Manufactured in the United States of America

Cover photo by Sylvia Dunnavant
Cover design by Creative Matters

Library of Congress Control Number: 00-133181

Special thanks to designer, Anthony Mark Hankins, for the use of his teapot and home for the cover photograph. Special thanks to Jessie Haynes.

ISBN 0-9667850-1-0

First Edition

Contents

Dedications

To my husband, Craig K. Smith, for being worth the sacrifice to create a happy marriage; and to the woman seeking a happy, love-filled marriage. I call you my girlfriend. And for you, I have taken the time to share my experiences.

Acknowledgements

To my Heavenly Father, thank You for Your inspiration and guidance in writing this book.

Thank You for my editor, Kim Wood, the loving hands You sent to prepare this work to Your glory.

Thank You for my publisher, Sylvia Dunnavant, the angel You sent to carry this work into the world.

Thank You, Father, for my husband, my eternal soul mate.

Thank You for my daughter, my love everlasting.

Thank You for my son, my joy forever.

Thank You for my mother, my rock in all lands.

Thank You for my father, my honor in all times.

Thank You for my only baby sister, my heart and Your voice in wary places.

Father, bless them.

I thank You for all those who have touched my life so far, for the journey has brought me to this place. Thank You.

Thank You for all those who have touched the making of this book in any good way. May they all be truly blessed.

Now, Father, I ask Your blessings and favor to be upon each person who buys and reads this book, and a double portion to those who spread the word of its existence to others. Father, may this book go forth in love and accomplish that which You initially intended. Amen.

Preface

I am writing this page after completing the one-hundred and eighteenth page of this book. In the beginning I was not going to have an introduction . . . just the preface, and then, my story. But I have to tell you something important right now. That's why I moved what was once my preface to become my introduction, and I'm going to use this page, the Preface, to get something straight . . . from the beginning.

You know how sometimes people will say something . . . make a statement about something only to find out later that it was not true or that something changed? Well, I want to go on record as saying that I don't know if Craig and I will be together for the rest of our lives. I don't know if we will get a divorce or separate after this book is published, on the market and in your hot little hands . . . I can't read into the future. But, what I can tell you is this: from our second year of marriage, until now, we have had a wonderful life together. Right now, all I can tell you is how I have managed to keep my good-looking, well-built, executive husband smiling and excited about coming home for over 23 years.

This book is not filled with "tricks of the trade," but rather with ways of being.

Introduction

"Abby's between girlfriends" was written for those of us who aren't willing to settle for a mediocre marriage. We need to feel loved. We want to be appreciated. Some would say we are "spoiled," but I say we just want to be cherished. During my 23 years of marriage, I have found many secrets to creating that loving relationship we long for, and I've never stopped searching for more of those treasured secrets. These pages were not only written to show women how to have a happy marriage, but also to show them how to be happy in a marriage.

Do you remember the biblical story of Leah, Rachel and Jacob in Genesis 29? I will never forget the day, a few Sundays ago, that Craig and I sat in church intensely listening to the story surrounding this love/hate triangle. I don't think I'll ever forget that day. I was enthralled by the story, which goes something like this:

Jacob loved Rachel so much that he made an agreement with her father to work for him for seven years to earn her hand in marriage. After seven long years (which Jacob said seemed to be but a few days to him) of working to have Rachel for himself, Rachel's father, Laban, tricked Jacob. Instead of getting Rachel all for himself, Laban deceitfully led Jacob into sleeping with his oldest daughter, Leah. Of course, with this accomplished, Jacob had to marry Leah.

Jacob hated Leah, but he loved the beautiful Rachel. He loved Rachel so much, that he agreed to work another seven years for Laban in exchange for her hand.

As I tuned my ears to the lecturer who continued to unravel the saga, Craig nudged my knee and passed me a note. The note said, "Thank you for being my Rachel."

Now . . . how can I explain to you the feelings that absorbed me? Oh, the feeling of knowing you are loved. The most wonderful feeling in the world — total joy.

I didn't always feel this way, though. When I thought about how I almost lost my marriage during our first year, I was moved to write the following pages, hoping to keep others from making the same mistakes. Not knowing a few secrets almost cost me great happiness, and I don't want that to happen to anyone else.

What I learned has brought me more love, more attention and more appreciation. If you need more from your marriage, what I have written is just for you. And what I have to tell you will be just between us.

Your girlfriend,

Abby

By wisdom a house is built, and by understanding it is established; and by knowledge the rooms are filled with all precious and pleasant riches.

Proverbs 24:3-4

Part 1

The Beginning

Our friends say we were meant to be together. They say we started out with all of the right ingredients. I admit, we were the best of friends and very much in love. But even with all that going for us, we still suffered during our first year of marriage. That is why I am so very grateful for the secrets I have learned since that first year. Yes, we started out with a lot of love, friendship and commitment, but still we almost never found what we have today.

What I have learned has been so important to building a good, lasting relationship. I call the secrets I have learned "My Simple Sacrifices." "Simple" because they do not take much time and they are so easy to do. And "Sacrifices" because they must be made in order to have a truly happy marriage.

Our Love Story

Craig and I grew up on the same street. Our courtship began early as we went together throughout the fifth, sixth and seventh grades. It was around that third year that I began asking my dad if I could go to the elementary football games to watch Craig play. I remember how much I enjoyed standing on the sideline and cheering for Craig alongside his mother, stepfather, sisters and brothers.

But after a few games, my dad put his foot down. I could hear the concern in his voice as he said, "You and Craig are too young to be getting so serious about each other. You two are going to have to stop seeing each other." It was hard to believe; he wanted us to break up. When I broke the news to Craig, it was a sad day for both of us, but we both agreed to do as my father had asked.

Over the next few years, we remained friends, but Craig kind of went his way in life and I went mine. In our teens, we both dated others, and I even fell in and out of what my mother called "puppy love" a couple of times.

Craig, on the other hand, now says he has never loved anyone else. I remember Craig coming on Saturdays to mow the yard for my dad then. He seemed so nervous when I answered the door. He now tells me that it was because he still loved me, but I had no idea how he felt at the time. Yeah, I guess you could say I was in my own little teenage world.

I graduated from high school the summer before Craig because I had earned enough extra credits. I was only sixteen at the time. My dad wanted me to wait until I was seventeen to go off to school, so I went to the local community college for a year.

After that first year of college, I was ready to spread my wings. The week before I was to leave home, my sister, Jackie, gave me a going-away party, and she invited all my friends and high school classmates. Craig came, too. We started talking, and he asked me to dance. I remember like it was yesterday. We danced and talked all night long. It was as if we were the only two at the party. By the time the night was over, he asked me for a date. I accepted, and that is where we started... again.

Craig wrote me every single day when I was away in college, and he called as much as possible – almost every day. We had a wonderful courtship, and after a two-year engagement, we had a small April wedding in my parents' home.

My Reality

Sometime along the end of our first year of marriage, I remember reading a magazine article about rating your marriage. The article ended with a rating scale. You've probably seen the kind. It was designed to help women like us decide if we have a good marriage or not. I remember reading the article and scanning through the rating scale, but I quickly dismissed the information as not being for me. For goodness' sake, I was happy.

About a week later, Craig and I were riding in the car enjoying some good conversation. Out of the blue, I asked him, "Do you think our first year of marriage has been good?" There was silence. I waited, and then he cautiously said, "It's been all right." I must have appeared totally dumbfounded, and I was.

"Craig, what do you mean 'all right'? You haven't enjoyed our first year together?"

I guess he could hear the urgency in my voice, because he pulled over to the side of the road. By this time, tears of unbelief were streaming down my cheeks. He stopped the car and turned to look at me. It was then that I saw the sadness in his face for the very first time. I sat there crying as he told me how he felt – that he could not be happy if things continued as they were.

Till this day, I do not think Craig realized that I did not have a clue as to what he was trying to tell me, but I could sense that he was relieved to get his feelings out in the open. What he was saying seemed so foreign to me, and I began to realize that I did not know anything about this man.

I wanted him to tell me what I needed to do – how I could "fix it." But he didn't know what to tell me.

"Doesn't he understand that I love him? Doesn't he know

that I am doing what I think is right? I thought I was a good wife. I thought we were happy." All this raced through my mind as he tried to explain, but my tears kept coming.

Finally, I heard him say, "Abby, I love you, and if it means I have to change to keep you then I will change. My only problem is that I am afraid if I change for you, you will look up one day and realize that you don't love the person I have become."

I had no words to respond. I was empty. Craig started the car again, and we rode home in silence.

Oh, I loved him so much, but I didn't know how to make him happy. I cried day and night for three days. I honestly did not know what to do or where to turn. I did not have a clue as to how to start trying to rebuild my marriage. I was so broken inside. All I felt was the darkness of being alone and helpless.

But sometime in those three days, I reached out to God. With tears in my eyes, I asked God to help me. I prayed, "Father God, I need help, and I don't know where else to turn. Father, I don't want an 'all right' marriage. I want my husband to be happy. I want to be happy. I want us to have a joyful life together. Father, I thought I knew what I was doing. I thought I knew how to be a good wife. Please help me, because I honestly don't know what to do."

I know God heard me, because he started redirecting my thoughts. I even found myself in a bookstore for the first time in my life. As a child and young adult, I did not like to read. I read only when necessary, and that was usually for school. But there I was in the self-help section of the store. I can honestly tell you that my life, my husband's life and our marriage have not been the same since that day. And ironically, you could now even classify me as a "bibliophile" – a lover and collector of books.

Over the years, I have come to understand just what Craig was trying to tell me about our troubled start as newlyweds. He wanted me to stop trying to change him, but instead love him just the way he was. And just as important, he wanted me to return to the fun-loving person I was when he decided he wanted to spend the rest of his life with me.

Because of my reading and research combined with more than 23 years of experience in developing a happy marriage, I am convinced that the secrets I have learned along the way, which I call Simple Sacrifices, are the keys to a joyful, fun-filled and lasting union.

I am not claiming to be the ultimate authority on marriage, nor do I claim to have a quick fix to marriages plagued with problems of abuse, alcohol, etc. What I am offering is some encouragement for my married friends who have found themselves in a rut. Maybe you're there now. Do you want to get out? Listen close, and I'll share with you what has worked for me. After all, what are friends for?

Simple Sacrifices

Of course, if you want to build a solid marriage, you must start with a good foundation – the Simple Sacrifices. I will show you how to incorporate the Simple Sacrifices into your own life, and you will enjoy watching your husband and your marriage come alive. And girlfriend, when your husband comes alive and enjoys living his life with you, guess who benefits? Undeniably, you! He will not be able to help but pour his love your way, and he'll see you as being one in a million. Trust me! Learning these eight secrets will be worth your while.

Simple Sacrifice #1:

Accept your man.

We all want to be accepted just as we are. But why do we find it easier to accept our girlfriends at face value than we do our own husband? Acceptance does not mean just tolerating or putting up with someone. Accepting your husband means loving him and trying to understand his ways of being himself. It means accepting him and all of his habits and intricacies that are unique to him.

The best way of showing your acceptance is to concentrate on the good qualities your husband possesses instead of nagging about everything he does wrong. We all know that no one is perfect, so why do we constantly put our men down? Why do we insist on making them feel like "bad little boys"? Our men do not need their mothers; they need acceptance from their wives.

Food for Thought: If your husband had a mistress, would he keep going back to her if she continuously complained about his habits or behavior? Would a mistress be understanding and accepting of him even to the point of catering to him? This is one of the ways the "other woman" gets her foot in the door.

If you want to see your husband start to come alive again, try accepting him with no strings attached.

Simple Sacrifice #2

Admire your man.

It seems like once we get married, we stop communicating with our husband about how we feel about him. We automatically assume he knows. As wives, we think they know that we love and admire our husband. After all, would we have married him if we didn't? Really though, when was the last time you showed admiration toward your husband? When was the last time you expressed your admiration of his character, deeds, commitment, choices, decisions, good looks, etc.? If it has been a long time, he probably thinks you are not very interested in him anymore, and that can make him insecure in your marriage.

Food for Thought: What were the things you admired about your husband when you were dating? If a single woman got to know your husband now, what are some of the things she would admire about him? Now that you remember what you admire about him, tell him before someone else has a chance.

Take the time to openly admire something about your husband every day. If you want to see him come alive, be truthful, but tell him something you admire about him each day.

Simple Sacrifice #3

Appreciate your man.

Showing appreciation to another human being is one of the simplest things a person can do. But when we get married, it is one of the first acts of kindness to go. We take our husband for granted, thinking it is his job or duty to do the things he does.

Showing appreciation takes action on our part. Saying "Thank you, I appreciate that;" a kiss or a smile; notes in his briefcase, suitcase or lunch kit; and messages on his voice mail at the office or home – there are so many ways to show appreciation. You can buy him something special and include a thank-you card. You can put his favorite candy bar on his pillow with a note.

Every now and then, after a long day, I will draw Craig a bubble bath complete with candles on each corner of the tub, soft music, telephone, evening paper and a glass of wine. Before I leave him to his quiet moment, I tell him, "Thank you for all you do. I love you." That always brings the biggest, warmest smile across his face.

Food for Thought: We get back what we give out. If you want to be appreciated, learn to show appreciation. What are some of the ways the "other woman" would show your husband how much she appreciated him? What would she do? What can you do?

Always let your husband know you appreciate him. Just remember, he does not have to do anything for you or anyone else. So when he does something for you – no matter how small –

acknowledge the deed by showing your appreciation. Watch your husband come alive as you begin to show your appreciation of him.

Simple Sacrifice #4

Adapt to your man.

If your husband works long hours, is out of town a lot, etc., cater to his lifestyle. Make his homecoming fun and exciting. Find ways to let him know you are happy he is home instead of making him feel guilty about being gone from home. Also, your home should be a place where your husband can rest and be himself.

Learn from your husband what he does and does not like. When he makes suggestions or has an idea about something or somewhere to go, try saying, "That's a great idea! Let's..." We wives put our husband's ideas and suggestions down when we say things like, "That sounds good, but..." Learn to follow your husband's lead. We did when we were dating him. We let him be "the man." What happened to change that?

Food for Thought: I know Craig does not want me to nag him, nor does he want me for his doormat. I enjoy bringing fun to our life together, and he returns the favor. If you and your husband were the last two people on earth, would he stay with you because he had to or because he wanted to? When you adapt to your husband's ways and needs, don't look at it as being forced to adapt. No woman should be forced to do anything she does not want to do. Instead, make a conscious choice to willingly cater to your husband's unique lifestyle, wants and needs.

Simple Sacrifice #5

Share yourself with your man.

This is the last Simple Sacrifice I will be sharing with you now, and I'm saving three more for later. This principle is the one that is important for us as wives if we want to be happy in our marriage. When we get married, we tend to give ourselves to our husband and children. After a few years, we find that we have lost or forgotten about ourselves. When you give somebody something, they have it and you do not. We must learn not to *give* ourselves to our family, but to *share* ourselves with them. When you share something, you still have some for yourself.

I remember asking everybody in the house his or her favorite color. After they told me, I waited but no one asked me mine. I was sure they did not care, but I said it anyway, "My favorite color is royal blue." Everybody kind of looked at me and went on about their business. Boy, did I feel dumb!

About a week later, my son came home with a picture he drew for me. He said, "Mama, I made this just for you. I colored it with your favorite color – royal blue." It did not matter that the whole picture – grass included – was royal blue. What mattered was that he was listening to me; he heard me. And what I like mattered to him. Whenever Craig takes me car shopping, he always points out the deep blue colors. And looking back through the years, I recall that my daughter always selects something blue when buying me presents.

Through these experiences and others, I have learned to just open up and share my own likes and dislikes with my family. I have found that when they know what I like, they try to find ways to please me. But most importantly, when I share myself (even when I think they do not want to hear it), it helps me stay in contact with the true me.

Food for Thought: Do your husband and family know your favorite color? Do your husband and family know where you would go if you had a choice of vacationing spots? Do they know what you would spend most of your time doing while on vacation? Now, this is a vacation you have selected for yourself and you are taking it by yourself. Just you! Do you even know the answers to these questions? If not, take time to find yourself. Rediscover who you are and then share yourself with your family. You will be surprised to find out how much they really want to know about the real you. Show them your humanity.

I have not given myself away; I have just shared a part of myself along the way. I am not just my husband's wife, nor am I just my kids' mom. I am eternal. I am me!

I want you to know that it is possible to have a great marriage. Knowledge is power. I could talk about marriage and happiness day and night.

I will tell you how I have incorporated the Simple Sacrifices and other ways of being into my own life and marriage. And I want you to know how to use the Simple Sacrifices in your own marriage. The Simple Sacrifices may sound simple, but they are the foundation for affair-proofing a marriage.

I am living proof that practicing the Simple Sacrifices, understanding the tricks of the "other woman" and knowing a few other techniques, which I will share with you later, can build a beautiful marriage.

My marriage has been truly blessed by the application of the Simple Sacrifices, and yours will be, too.

Part 2

Laying a Firm Foundation

The Right Ingredient

When friends and others see Craig and me together, they think life for us is so easy. They comment on how happy we are with each other and how happy we are with life. They have the false notion that everything is always ideal for us.

What I want you to know is that Craig and I have had some tough times in our almost 23 years of marriage. The lessons I have learned about being happy in my marriage have come through living some of those tough times. Some of the life situations that have caused others to separate and even divorce have served to bring Craig and me closer together.

I want to share some of our joys and trials with you. I want you to see that it is not the situations you find yourself in that make your life what it is. It is the attitude with which you approach your marriage and life in general that makes life enjoyable.

I will definitely show you how I have applied the Simple Sacrifices to my marriage. But first, I want you to take a journey with me down Memory Lane. I want to take you back to the early years and bring you up to date with our life together. Throughout this journey, I want you to look for attitude, desire and faith.

Attitude, desire and faith are the key ingredients that give our marriages substance. When I talk to friends and others about marriage, most seem to desire a good, happy marriage. What I usually find lacking is the wife's right attitude or outlook about her husband, her marriage and even her life as a whole. Her thoughts are down and negative, so the words and phrases she uses are down and negative. When a person thinks negative thoughts and uses negative words, she paints herself into a negative world. It is impossible to have a negative outlook and have faith at the same time.

Let's journey back to the beginning of my marriage, and I'll show you how my attitude toward life situations and family matters, my strong desire to have a wonderful marriage and my faith in God have been the foundation on which my marriage stands.

When you have a firm foundation of attitude, desire and faith, the Simple Sacrifices serve as the interior design. The Simple Sacrifices will bring added comfort, joy, excitement, coziness and variety to your marriage.

Read this note Craig passed to me a few Sundays ago while I was ushering at church.

Abby,

There was a man by the name of Nabal whose wife was a woman of good reason and understanding. Nabal was a ruffian – a man who did not have good reason. Little did he know, his wife saved his life and his possessions. He did not know (truly) what he had. Unlike Nabal, I know exactly what I have. I love and adore you. You are the most beautiful woman I have ever laid my eyes on.

I love you,

Craig

I know I am living what some women only dream of, and I truly thank God. But girlfriend, it hasn't always been this way. It has been a long, hard journey getting to this point.

Flying High

By the time we were 21, Craig and I owned and operated Smith Delivery Service. Our primary clients were interior designers, owners of antique showrooms and furniture designers in and around Dallas' World Trade Center, which is a major market hub located near the city's downtown area.

Craig handled the pick-up and delivery of furniture and paintings to and from some of the finest homes and businesses in the area. I answered the telephone, scheduled deliveries and provided customer service, and I handled all office duties from bookkeeping to payroll.

We had four full-time employees, a couple of two-ton trucks and one cargo van. We grossed $89,000 our second year in business. In our third year, we picked up an account that caused us to expand and move from our home-based office to an office and a warehouse.

We also handled a lot of warehousing and distribution for another office furniture and supply company. Our business grew so much that we had to buy another van and hire two more full-time employees to handle the demands of that account.

That one account paid all our bills, both personal and business. It paid everything from the house note to employee wages. All of our other deliveries and commercial moves were gravy.

During those early years of business, we were already raising our two babies. Chloé was three and Clayton was one year old. We were in our second home and could afford life's necessities, and a lot of the extras. We were living large.

My only complaint was that since both of us worked in the business, that was all we seemed to talk and think about. Craig would take me out to dinner, and we would spend the evening discussing the business. To me, that was the only downfall to being self-employed... that and the fact that when anything went wrong, it fell squarely on our shoulders, and we had to take the load until we resolved the situation. We didn't have the luxury of looking to someone else like our employees had. But that was all a part of the freedom of being our own boss: handling the responsibilities, you know?

Hard Times

In spite of our apparent success, by the time we turned 25, Craig and I filed bankruptcy. In the early eighties, the economy was weak, but that wasn't what caused our decline – not at first.

As I said before, we were flying high. Craig was at our major account doing a little PR when the warehouse manager mentioned to him that their vice president was moving his office to Dallas. He wanted us to handle the delivery and set-up of furniture and paintings for his new office.

Because of all the daily demands of that one account along with our other clients, we were short of manpower. We had two weeks to decide how we were going to handle the move. We seemed to be growing so fast, yet we did not feel it was time to hire another full-time employee. So Craig decided to rent another truck, which we did from time to time, and he hired a guy from a well-known temporary agency in town. Craig took our most experienced employee off his usual route and put him in the rental truck as the driver alongside the temporary worker. Craig took our employee's place for the day.

Later on that evening, Craig made it back home saying all the deliveries had gone smoothly. Then the telephone rang. It was the warehouse manager of our major account, so I gave the phone to Craig. All I can remember was hearing him say, "Why?" When he hung up the telephone, he just sat there. "What is it?" I asked. He just sat there. "Craig, what is it?"

"We lost the account."

"Why?"

"I don't know. The warehouse manager just said that the vice president called him downstairs and told him that he did not want Smith Delivery Service to ever step foot on their property again."

We both just sat there in silence for a long time. I think I saw tears in Craig's eyes. I cannot be sure because my eyes were full of them, too.

We found out later that the vice president said something to the young temporary worker while our employee was getting something from the truck. Whatever was said, the temporary worker took offense and cursed at the vice president. Oh, the difference a day makes.

We hung in there for another year, but our other accounts were not strong or steady enough to sustain us in those bad economic times. When we finally decided to close up shop, Craig found jobs around town for our full-time employees. He called the different businesses personally, explained what was happening and gave each one of our employees recommendations over the telephone. When we called the guys in to tell them that we were going to have to file bankruptcy, he had job offers already lined up for each one. That's the kind of man Craig is.

At that time we did not even have the $1500 to hire a lawyer to handle our bankruptcy. We were both without jobs, and all of our savings were gone. We were 24 and a half years old and scared to death.

The Light

One Saturday morning, I was washing dishes and the telephone rang. It was another bill collector demanding payment. I was at my wits' end, just wanting to scream. I did not know where to turn, and I felt the pressure coming from everywhere. No job, no money, bills, babies and two adults clinging to each other. Just holding on... holding on for dear life.

Girlfriend, you don't know what scared is until you look down at your babies' innocent and trusting faces and wonder where their next meal will come from; or when you look up into your husband's eyes and see him asking for forgiveness because he does not know what to do. Scared, girl... I'm talking about *scared.*

I slammed the telephone down, not wanting to hear another word the bill collector had to say. Instead, I went back to the sink to finish washing the dishes.

The kids were napping, and Craig had gone across town for something. That's when the tears came without warning. I was standing there washing dishes and crying uncontrollably. Almost without consciousness, I said, "Jesus, I have heard about you all of my life. If you are real, please come into my life."

Somewhere in there, I acknowledged being a sinner and asked for forgiveness. I admitted that my life was in a mess. All I could say was, "Help me, I don't know where else to turn." Now, I can't tell you exactly what happened then. All I know is my hands had come out of the water and were stretched toward heaven.

As the dishwater ran down my arms and the tears ran down my cheeks, warmth and light filled my whole body. As I was bringing my hands down, I felt a peace that calmed every part of me. Before my hands reached the dishwater, the telephone rang. I quickly dried my hands, arms and face.

Still feeling that sweet peace, I answered the telephone. It was my "uncle."

My mother and his wife were roommates in college. They are just like sisters, so we have always called her Aunt Jerry and him Uncle Charles.

Now, this was the first time he had ever called my house, so I was caught a little off guard.

"Are you all right?" he asked.

"Yes, sir."

"Tell me now... tell the truth. I heard y'all were having some financial problems over there. Is that true?

"Yes, sir."

"How much do you need?"

I did not know what to say. The house note was a couple of months behind, the kids needed shoes and we needed food. "Four hundred to five hundred dollars," I said, thinking that was too much to ask for, but knowing it was still not enough.

"Y'all come over tomorrow, and that will give your Aunt Jerry time to go to the bank. We'll have it for you."

When I hung up that telephone, girl, I was so thankful!

About an hour later, my mother called and I started telling her about the telephone conversation with Uncle Charles and she said, "I know. I was there."

Mom had gone over to my aunt's house to visit. While they were talking, my mother mentioned that I was keeping my weight down pretty good. (That's a big thing in our family, because we are all on the heavy side. I have weighed as much as 215 pounds, and Craig has never once complained. I think that is one of the reasons I work so hard on maintaining a healthy weight. I know Craig loves me fat or slim, so I do what I do strictly for me. No one is harder on us than we are on ourselves.)

Anyway, my mother told my Aunt Jerry that it was probably because of everything I was going through. Well, my Uncle Charles overheard the conversation and asked my mom what was going on. My mother told them about our business failing. And she also told them that for the first time in a long time, she and my daddy were financially strapped and couldn't help out much.

That is when my Uncle Charles went to the telephone and asked, "What's their phone number?" All I could think was that you have to give God a hand for timing!

Before I could get off the telephone with my mother, Craig walked in. When I hung up, he looked at me and said, "Baby, we're going to make it. I was on my way home, and I couldn't take it anymore. I just pulled over under the bridge and cried. But I know now that God is going to take care of us. I know He heard my cry."

We stood there and held each other for a long time. Then I told him what had happened to me and about the telephone conversation with Uncle Charles. We held each other some more; we just held on, girl. But the holding was different – there was hope mixed in there somewhere.

The next day we went to pick up the money from Uncle Charles and Aunt Jerry. He gave me the envelope and told me that it was not a loan. He said it was our money, and we didn't owe him anything. A long time ago, my father helped him and Aunt Jerry when they needed it most, and Uncle Charles said he felt like this was his chance to pay him back by helping his child.

I opened the envelope and there was $1000 inside! I wanted to cry so badly. Oh, I was so relieved and so very thankful. Uncle Charles said experience had taught him that people only ask for half of what they really needed.

Craig and I caught the house note back up, but we let one of our cars go back. Actually, when the dealership sold the car, they made $89 over the loan balance and mailed us a check for that amount. We stocked up on groceries and bought each of the kids a few clothes and a new pair of shoes.

I don't think I will ever forget the warm light that flooded my body when I invited Jesus into my life. I stayed in that state of peace and understanding for a long time. I think we as Christians spend the rest of our lives trying to recapture the initial feeling of surrender – when we truly surrendered it all. I felt so pure inside. It was like being washed and made clean. It was like being loved and knowing I was forgiven for any and everything I had ever done. I felt so new, so different, so complete. . . so loved.

I did not want to make love for about three days. I just did not want to be touched in that way. I did not want to lose that pure feeling. I'm glad I experienced that feeling first, because a couple of years later when Craig had his religious encounter, he did not want to make love for three days also. I understood what he was going through. I just didn't want to lose that wonderful pure feeling, and my body seemed to just naturally reject the notion of sex. I guess it's the process of renewing that takes place. But after those three days, He restoreth me! Amen? A-m-e-n!

I started reading my Bible daily. At first, it was hard for me because the Bible seemed so difficult to read, but I went to the bookstore and bought a translated version – the New International Version (NIV) to be exact. After buying a Bible I could understand, I really grew to enjoy my daily reading. Sometimes it seemed like I could not get enough. I felt so close to God; I felt like He understood everything I was going through. I knew I had someone to lean on, and I came to realize that God was always there. He was always in my life. The important thing was that I had finally acknowledged His presence. I know He is with me, I know He is all-powerful and I know He will make a way for me. Like the old folks used to say, "He'll make a way out of no way!"

Bankruptcy

Craig and I were taking turns going out to look for jobs. We could not afford daycare for the kids, so one of us had to stay home. I was the first to find a job, and it paid $4 per hour. Craig found one two weeks later making $4.25 an hour. Even with the new jobs, we could not handle all the bills we had acquired while we were in business, and we still could not afford a lawyer.

We knew we were going to have to do something, so we decided to file bankruptcy without a lawyer. We called the county to find out what we needed to do, and that mainly consisted of filling out lots of paperwork.

When we finished that chore, Craig took the papers downtown to the county where he was given a case number. When the bill collectors called, we gave them our case number and that was that.

Our court date finally came. Oh, we were so nervous; we just did not know what to expect. And we were so young, but we were braving the big bad world anyway.

On the way to court, we dropped the kids off at my great aunt's before stopping at the elementary school where my mother was a counselor. She met us at the back door for a moment. As we walked back to the car, I felt a quaking inside me. I knew at that moment that my mother was just as nervous for us as we were for ourselves, but I also felt her prayers.

Our next stop was the courthouse. We parked and walked to the building, hand in hand all the way. Just as we were about to enter the courtroom, Craig pulled me back and took me around the corner. He grabbed both my hands and prayed like I had never heard him pray before. When he finished, we both looked at each other and with our eyes we said, "Okay, let's go."

Our Lawyer

The courtroom was packed. As we looked around, it seemed as if we were the only ones without a lawyer. I was already nervous, but when I saw how harsh the judge was with the couple before us, you could have picked me up off the floor. With one look at him, it was obvious that he had a low tolerance level. The couple before us looked like all they wanted to do was get out of there.

"Next." We were up. While the judge was looking down at our bankruptcy documents and asking if we were represented by counsel, we approached the bench through the two short swinging doors. "No, sir," we replied.

With that said, he brought his head up to look at us. Girlfriend, listen, I saw that judge's eyes change like night changing to day. I mean to tell you that I looked at that man with disbelief. Listen, those were not the same eyes I had just seen a few minutes before when he was speaking to the couple in front of us. These eyes were soft and filled with compassion. Why, they almost had a sparkling glaze, a kind of light to them. Oh, girl! I wish I could describe those eyes for you, but I just can't find the words. It was shattering. I knew his physical body was the same outside, but I also knew that something was occurring on the inside of that man. He kind of squirmed just a little; seemed like maybe he was caught off guard or something. But he quickly regained his composure and proceeded.

The judge asked us a question – one of those questions our lawyer would have been paid to know how to answer, if we had one. Craig and I kind of half looked at each other, not knowing what to say.

The judge could tell by the look on our faces that we did not have a clue as to how we should answer his question, so he answered it for us. I'm telling you, girlfriend, that man became our judge and our lawyer in that courtroom, right there in front of all those other people and their own lawyers.

We only had one creditor show up at the hearing, and I could tell by the look on his face that he was just as dumbfounded as we were. He went along with the judge, and they worked out everything – the two of them – while Craig and I just stood there.

Girl, when I say all we had to do was stand there, that's exactly what I mean. We just stood there while our "lawyer-judge" took care of us.

When they finished talking back and forth, our "lawyer-judge" turned his attention back to us. He was dismissing us to leave. I remember that look in his eyes that said, "I've taken care of it for you. You can go now." I felt just like a well-cared-for child. He didn't smile. He just looked with those merciful eyes.

I was so caught up in the moment, I actually forgot there were other people in the room. When Craig and I turned to leave, I saw that every eye in that courtroom, lawyers' included, was on us. As we exited the courtroom door, I could hear our "lawyer-friend-judge" call, "N-e-x-t."

On our way back to the car, we held each other in relief. It was as if the weight of the world had been lifted off our shoulders. After we were both back in the car and on our way, I said, "Did you see those eyes?"

"Yes," he said softly.

"No, Craig, I am talking about that man's eyes. Did you see his eyes change?"

"Yes, Abby, I saw his eyes change," he said so very seriously. "It was Jesus."

By that time, tears – tears of humble joy – had moistened my own eyes. I looked at Craig and said, "Jesus must really love us to come all the way down from heaven to take care of us."

"Yeah, you're right."

I will never – not ever – forget those eyes. Jesus placed His spirit in that judge not only to be our lawyer in the courtroom, but also to prove His love for us.

The Sweetest Sound

There have been other instances that let me know that life is much more than what we see with our human eyes. Just a few years after the courtroom incident, I had another enlightening experience. That morning, the house was nice and quiet – the perfect time to enjoy a day off from work. I was stretched out across my bed reading a good book when I got a craving for something from the kitchen. I got up and headed that way, but as I was about to pass through the bedroom door, I heard this music – really soft music.

"Hmm, I must have left the radio on," I thought to myself. So, I reached on top of the armoire to cut the radio off, but to my surprise, it was not on. Girl, I just froze in place. And as I stood there, the music became louder, but never too loud. I cannot explain it. All I can tell you is that I believe in the heavenly choir. I was surrounded by the sweetest voices I have ever heard. I stood there for a few minutes engulfed in the sound before it faded away just as softly as it came.

My Guardian Angel

And going back to my childhood, I recall another special moment. Even at age 12, I knew that there was more – much more – to life than we will ever know on earth.

Let me paint a mental picture of that day. There we were, a car full of ladies (some older than others) on our way to the beauty shop. In the front seat was my great aunt – a beautician by trade. Beside her in the driver's seat was one of her customers. My younger sister by 14 months sat in the backseat with me, and my great aunt's granddaughter was sandwiched between the two of us.

There we went down Ledbetter Avenue. I was sitting back, just kind of staring out the front window, peeping between my great aunt and the driver. Then, all of a sudden, I realized I was looking ahead at nothing. It was as though a grayish, unpleated curtain veiled the front windshield from outside.

A voice inside me said, "Be still. Do not be afraid." Then that voice took shape and seemed to swoop out from the back of my head. It went around to my left, coming out just far enough forward for me to see it with my peripheral vision. It was white with a round, bubble-shaped head. I saw no eyes, no mouth nor any other human features. It was just a smoky white, round form about the size of a grapefruit. Oh, and it had a thick stem that allowed it to stretch from inside my head, out the back and around to my left side. I have come to call that being my guardian angel.

It seemed to understand me totally and consoled me, saying, "You are going to feel one bump, and then you will turn around two times. You will hit one more time, and then it will be over." With these words spoken, it disappeared back around my head with the same swooping sound.

I still could not see out of the front windshield. But sure enough, I felt one bump followed by another bump a few seconds later. Later at the scene of the car accident, witnesses explained how the vehicle struck the median and turned around twice in the street before hitting a cement wall.

As I was getting out of the car, I could hear my sister screaming, "I can't get out! Help me! Please, somebody! I can't get out." At her cry, I snapped to my senses, jumped out of the car and ran around to her door to help. No matter how hard I tried, I just could not get the door open. Before I knew it, several men came to my aid and pried it open. My sister, my cousin and I were okay. The driver hurt herself on the steering wheel, but she came through all right. My great aunt hit her head on the windshield, and she also broke her hip. To this day, she still walks with a limp.

But the injuries could have been much more serious. I remember seeing our wreck on the ten o'clock news and realizing how bad it really was. The hood of the car was crushed into the front seat when the car hit the retaining wall.

Now, you tell me. How would my guardian angel know what was going to happen, exactly as it was going to happen before it actually happened unless. . . well, unless it knows the future? Now, don't you think that if it knows the future, it probably knows the present as well as the past? And another thing, my guardian angel did not come flying from somewhere, nor did it fly away. It came from somewhere inside of me. And it went back to where it came from when it was finished giving instructions – back inside of me.

Over the years, this one incident has given me solace in different situations. I am still learning to follow my inner feelings, knowing when to do or say something and when to hold back. I truly believe that there is a guide inside of me that knows what is going to happen. I believe it loves me, it leads me and it steers me from trouble and guides me to happiness if I take heed to its directions – those feelings from within.

So, when I say, "I know that there is a God, and we cannot see everything with the natural eye, but that does not mean it's not there," you can understand what I'm saying and why I'm saying it.

Mutual Trust

Through the failure of our business, never once did I blame Craig. I understood that we were both learning things as life went along. I also knew that each decision we made had the possibility of working out right or working out wrong. Without a doubt, Craig has always loved the kids and me, and he makes each decision with our best interests at heart. If for some reason the outcome was not what we wanted, I stepped in and showed him my love even more.

Many wives or husbands when facing financial crises play the blame game. They point fingers instead of remaining partners. I always try to let Craig know that I stand behind him no matter what. I believe my expression of trust early in our marriage helped Craig strengthen his self-confidence with regard to decision-making.

Knowing that I will be with him even through the hard times has also deepened his trust in me.

Lighten Up

Yeah, when our business failed, our combined take-home pay was so small that we had to put ourselves on a strict budget. You know how people say they live from paycheck to paycheck? Well, we lived from paycheck to *before* paycheck. We had very little to allow for groceries each week. That meant that I could not buy some of Craig's favorite food items like Blue Bell™ Ice Cream, Miracle Whip™ Sandwich Spread and even honey. These were the main three he missed, and it hurt me not to be able to buy them.

But Craig went shopping with me each week. He was better than me about buying in bulk and stretching our little bit of grocery money. I loved going to the grocery store with Craig. He always made it fun, and we never went over our budget when he was with me.

He did not think twice about being unable to afford his favorite foods (or at least he did not show any signs). And all brand name items, unless on sale, were out.

No matter what we go through, I try to make the best of the situation we are in, and make it pleasurable. Pleasure is important to a man. "Other women" use the lure of fun and folly to trap a man who is bored from routine and worries. That is one of the reasons some men seek younger women who appear to offer pleasure and enjoyment. Notice I said, "appear." What he sees isn't always what he gets!

Seek for Joy

We ran into many obstacles in those early days after the bankruptcy. Each utility was cut off at least twice within the year. One evening, the electricity was off when we got home from work, and we couldn't get it turned back on until the next day when we were able to get some money.

I prayed, "God, what can I do to make this an enjoyable evening? I need your help." I just knew He would help me like I asked. I truly believe God honors the family, and if you put your family second only to Him, He will honor your requests for help and bring joy into your home. I really believe that. The only thing is this: you have to be ready to do what He says. You cannot ask God for help and then be too lazy to act on His direction when He answers you.

So, just how did God help me put some electricity back in our home that evening? Well, I gathered up some candles and heated up the gas range in our little two-bedroom, gingerbread-style home. I cooked a big dinner in the light of dusk. By nightfall, I spread the candles throughout the house and lit every one of them. Then Craig and I, along with the kids, sat down to a beautifully set dinner table, shimmering from the glow of the candles.

I made sure the conversation was light-hearted and fun. The four of us sat around the dinner table, eating and smiling, talking and listening to each other and laughing together for more than an hour.

As we were finishing dinner and preparing to clear the table, the doorbell rang. Craig pushed back from the table, wiping his mouth with his white linen napkin. (I told you, I went all out! Everything I needed to have a beautiful evening was already there. I just had God's help in remembering what I already had and how to use it for the occasion.) Anyway, Craig excused himself and went to the door. He announced, "It's Mama."

Now girl, we really didn't let our families know a lot about the struggles we were going through. One of my teachers in college told me before I was married not to run to my parents with everything. She said, "If you are hungry when you visit, just go to the refrigerator and get something to eat. But don't tell your parents all of your business, because they love you too much to stay out of your way."

She also warned, "It is hard enough for parents to let their children go, and when you keep them involved in everything you do, it is hard for them to view you as a capable adult. Then, when the problem finally straightens itself out, your parents will still view you as their child and not as the adult that you are."

So, there we were with Craig's mother at the door. I could hear her saying as they moved through the house back toward the dining room, "Well, I've been trying to call you for two or three days, and the telephone is still disconnected. I've been a little worried about y'all, so I thought I would just come on over and make sure everything is all right."

"Hi, Mama," I said as she entered the dining room.

"Hi, dear," she replied.

While our plates were empty and ready to be removed from the table, the candles were still flickering beautifully, and anyone would have realized that we were enjoying a wonderful evening. I invited her to fix a plate, but she said, "No. I just stopped by to check on y'all and make sure everything is okay and to see if you need anything."

"Oh, no, Mama, we're fine." Craig said, "We'll probably have the phone turned back on next week, but we'll have the lights back on tomorrow." With us checked on, she decided to be on her way. As she was on her way out the door, she said, "If you need me, call me."

We gave the kids a bath and tucked them both into bed, and Craig and I were in bed before nine o'clock, snuggling and giggling. As we dozed off to sleep, he said, "Baby, I'm the luckiest man in the world." Hearing those words made it all worth the sacrifice.

The kids really enjoyed their candlelight evening. In fact, the next night, Clayton wanted to turn off the lights and burn the candles again. Of course, Craig wanted to turn the television off and call it another early night, if you know what I mean.

Find the Joy

You know, sometimes it seems like it would be easier to give up, walk around angry and blame everyone and everything for our problems. Sometimes, it seems simplest to wallow in self-pity and gloom. Let me tell you something; it takes courage to stand, and it takes strength to be positive when there is so much darkness lurking around. If you do choose to put forth that extra effort to be positive, you will reap the benefits in the end. You will keep the channel open for positive things to come into your life. Remember, you reap what you sow. Sow a positive outlook, then reap positive returns in your life. But if you choose to take the easy way out by just giving up and giving in to gloom, this attitude could likely lead to depression and illness. Don't give in to the negative self-talk. Instead, fight within yourself to remain positive, because it is worth the fight. I try to remember the old saying, "Joy is the elixir of life." And the best place to find joy is in the presence of God.

I truly believe this is one of the secrets to developing deep love in a relationship. Remember, God made each of us. He knows what we are made of, and He knows what makes each of us happy. Most people don't fully understand one other, but God knows us inside out and wants to bless our marriages. If we earnestly seek God to teach us to accept love and to show love, then He is ready to pour out His guidance. God never forces Himself on us, so remember to invite Him into your marriage.

Simple Pleasures

As the months passed, Craig and I started getting small raises in pay from our jobs. I was able to occasionally buy Miracle Whip™, Blue Bell™ Ice Cream and honey for Craig. I could not buy them very often, but that didn't matter. He made that stuff s-t-r-e-t-c-h. Girl, it's a wonderful thing to be thankful and appreciative from the inside out. You should have been a fly on the wall to watch him eat his spoonfuls of vanilla heaven. Craig appreciated his Miracle Whip and his honey in the same way.

Speaking of appreciation, about a year after the bankruptcy, I realized that after paying the bills, we had some extra money.

"Craig, we have an extra ten dollars here. What do you want to do with it?" He looked at me for a second and then said, "Let's go to the mall and buy something special for the house." Let me tell you, we got dressed and dressed the kids so fast, it would have made your head spin. Out the door and off to the mall we went.

We had so much fun trying to find something with that ten dollars. You would have thought we were the Beverly Hillbillies coming to the city for the first time. We looked from floor to ceiling in those stores with smiles on our faces. When I caught myself, I realized that we hadn't been to the mall or any department store in over a year. The thought kind of made me sad inside, but I was glad to be there.

We ended up buying a beautiful crystal ashtray for the living room cocktail table. The ashtray was for a habit we have both long since given up.

Then the big moment came – the moment when we were able to walk into the store and buy both our kids a pair of shoes without help from anyone else. I will never forget that feeling of genuine joy, and certainly no part of that blessing was taken for granted. By the time the salesman brought the shoes for the kids to try on, I was fighting back humbling tears.

Through all of that, Craig was working a regular job with two, sometimes three, odd jobs on the side. Some Saturdays when we needed extra money, Craig would gather up some number stencils and black spray paint. With me and the kids in the car, Craig would go to different neighborhoods and offer to spraypaint street numbers on the curb for $10 a house. Some homeowners would say no, but a lot of them would oblige. After bringing in $40 or $50 for that day, which usually took a couple of hours, Craig would say, "Now, let's go get some groceries." Between that and Craig's early morning job delivering newspapers, I knew that he was with me through thick and thin.

I don't think Craig has ever had to wonder if I would run out on him when things get tough. Women do that too, you know? But on the other hand, he has never taken me for granted. Craig knows that I have a choice, and the choice I have made is to be with him, through the good times and the bad.

Digging out of our financial dilemma took quite a while. After years of depending on my father to co-sign on car loans, we were finally able to make big purchases like this on our own.

Give God What's His

It wasn't long after we hit the hard times when my sister expressed her concern regarding whether Craig and I tithe. I looked at her and said, "Girl, we can't even pay our bills. How are we going to be able to afford to give ten percent of our income to the church?" With eyes of gentle compassion, she looked at me and explained, "If you only have ten dollars, you can't pay your bills with it anyway. What would you lose by putting a tenth – just one dollar – in the church?" I knew in my mind that she had a point, but I couldn't manage to get that out my lips.

Since I never answered her, my sister thought I didn't get the message. "Where is your Bible?" she asked. I went to the bedroom to get my Bible, with her following close behind. I picked the Bible up from the nightstand and handed it to her, and she then flipped over to the third chapter of Malachi. My baby sister handed that Bible back to me and said, "Here, now read verses 10 and 11."

Now listen, this was my only sister – my baby sister. It's funny how she was the one to remind me what we were taught as children. But that woman saved our financial life that day. I read those two verses and understood that if we paid our tithes, God would bless us abundantly and would watch over us and our livelihood. Well, Craig and I have been tithing ever since that day. And I can tell you, "God's Word does not come back void." You know, He tells us that in Isaiah 55:11.

I have learned two things about tithing since those early days, and these two things have really opened up the windows of heaven even more. While we used to tithe only on our take-home pay, for the last few years we have been tithing on our gross income. We decided to follow the lead of a wealthy, brilliant Christian businessman that we know. This local business owner is well-respected, and he has always given Craig good, sound advice. Craig and I agreed to heed his wise counsel, and we have been tithing on our gross income ever since. The second thing I've learned is to pay my tithe to a place that is helping others – a place that has a positive vision.

We are presently members of a church that has over 100 ministries and outreach programs. I can tell you this, God has truly blessed us, and Craig and I are so thankful. When you tithe on fertile ground – that is, at a place where God's work is being done by feeding the poor, helping the widows and the fatherless, giving care to the needy, and so on – then you are being God's hands and feet. You are someone who God is using to reach His people.

I have read in several places that financial problems, death in the family and infidelity are the three main causes of divorce. However, our financial problems brought us closer than ever. But remember, we never blamed each other for the poor circumstances. We just endured the hard times and made it through them together.

Even when we first started tithing on our gross income, it was a major adjustment. We stayed prayerful and committed together, and it has paid off. Our businessman friend knew what he was talking about. When you tithe on your all and make sure it goes to help those in need, God opens the windows of Heaven and continues to pour out His blessings.

Forgive as You Are Forgiven

Once Jesus showed me how much He loves me, I think His next order of business was to teach me about forgiveness.

I was sitting in bed reading my Bible some years ago when I came across the Gospel of Mark 11:25-26. "And when ye stand praying, forgive if ye have ought (grudge) against any: that your Father also which is in heaven may forgive you your trespasses. But if ye do not forgive, neither will your Father which is in heaven forgive your trespasses." I just kind of laid my head back and pondered on those two verses. That was the first time that I really knew, down in my heart, that I did not want to harbor a grudge against anyone. However, I really didn't feel as though I was holding any grudges.

As I reclined in my bed, I just kept thinking. Then, guess whose face popped into my mind? That guy – the one that caused us to lose our major account! Once I pictured his face in my mind, along came this flood of negative emotions. It actually startled me. I mean, I had not realized until then that I was holding a grudge against that young man. I prayed,

"Lord, if I didn't even realize I was holding this grudge, how in the world can I stop myself from feeling this way about him? I need your help, so please show me what to do." Well, let me tell you, in the course of that week, I had my answer. God reminded me that Jesus should be my example. He forgave me of all my sins, and that is the way I should forgive that young man. I needed to just forgive him, and I did.

You see, God can bring good out of a bad situation. If that young man had not played the part in my life that he did, I would not have personally met the Lord as early as I did. Craig and I would not be as close as we are today. For that matter, I might not have gone back to college to finish my B.A. degree, and I might not have gotten certified as a special education teacher, which has given me my own career. That young man actually brought many blessings my way.

Since that revelation in bed, I regularly go back and examine my heart for bitterness. I think of the different people in my life, one by one. If a negative feeling comes up, then I ask God to help me to forgive that person. And I believe those feelings will go away, and they do. Usually, when I think of that same person about a week later, there is a feeling of kindness inside. That is when I can truly thank God for the victory. After all, He did it – not me.

Listen, if you want to experience true freedom, try walking this earth without having a harsh feeling toward anyone. Not only will you benefit, but so will your husband. Your husband will enjoy a sweeter you – a you who is not bogged down with unresolved grudges from the past.

Striving for a Pure Heart

In addition to my regular check for bitterness, I do a similar exercise I call, "Yes, Lord." You know, sometimes in life, things and people can become too important to us. God is a jealous God, and He does not want anything nor anyone to be more important to us than Him. So every once in a while, I do this exercise. I visualize someone (Craig, my daughter or my son) or something (my house, my car, etc.). As I hold the image in my mind, I ask myself, "Would you give this up for God?" I then wait for my heart to answer, "Yes,

Lord." If I experience a gnawing feeling in my heart, then I know I am placing more importance on that person or that thing than I should. You know, your mouth may say one thing, but your heart cannot lie.

When I first started this exercise, I asked myself if I put Craig before God. Sure enough, I felt that tugging feeling at my heart. I knew right then and there that I had placed Craig too high in my life. As much as I love him, he still should not come before God in my mind and in my heart. Tearfully, I prayed for forgiveness. "Yes, Lord." I don't want to ever put anyone or anything above God. Craig could die or leave me for another woman, but who is always going to be there for me? God, that's who. My kids could be killed, get kidnapped or grow up to disappoint me terribly. Who's going to always be there for me? God, that's who. My house could burn down; my car could be wrecked. Who's going to see me through it all? God, that's who. I do my very best to keep God number one in my life.

I believe this is one of the reasons Craig is still attracted to me. Craig knows that my love is not a desperate love. He knows that I love him and want to be with him, but I do not need him and I can make it without him. When Craig sees me walk in the door or climb in bed, he knows I am where I want to be, and let me tell you, that's a powerful love potion. We are two whole people, loving each other fully.

Great Faith

I don't exactly know when Jesus started working with me in the area of having faith in God. Sometime during those difficult years after the bankruptcy, God started convicting me in the area of having stronger faith in Him. Hebrews 11:6 says, "But without faith, it is impossible to please Him." And verse one of the same chapter says, "Now faith is the substance of things hoped for, the evidence of things not seen." See? It is right there.

I'm telling you, the Lord took those verses and helped me build my future around their meaning. I remember asking, "Lord, how do I have faith? How do I practice this kind of faith? Lord, show me how to use my faith; I want to please God." And that's where it all started. All I had to do was ask.

Once I asked for guidance on building my faith, God led me to certain books and drew me to certain people. The first book I read on the subject was "Secret of the Ages" by Robert Collier. I discussed Collier's theories with my father.

My dad said that everything significant he has done in life came after reading that book. In addition to this book, I have read many other books on the subject of faith. They all come back to one key point: "Faith is the substance of things hoped for, the evidence of things not seen." Okay, now listen; let me break it down to you. First, let me show you something right here in the Bible. I base the power behind my faith on these verses. John 16:23-24 says, "And in that day ye shall ask me nothing. Verily, verily, I say unto you, whatsoever ye shall ask the Father in my name, He will give it to you." Jesus goes on to say, "Hitherto have ye asked nothing in my name. Ask, and ye shall receive, that your joy may be full."

"Ask, and ye shall receive." That is what I hold onto as a promise to me from God, and it is the springboard for my faith.

When there is something I want, the first thing I do is go to the Lord in prayer. I ask God for whatever it is I want in the name of Jesus, and I ask Him to grant my desire if it is within His will for me. I know He only wants the best for His children. In this way, I have made known the desires of my heart, and I have asked for divine help in obtaining my desire.

I call the next thing I do "faith work." Since I already know God is going to grant me my desire if it is right for me, I visualize what I want just as I want it to be. Some people call it "seeing with the mind's eye," but I look at it as taking a photo of what I want and keeping it in my mind. While I have the image in my mind, I stir up the feelings right then – the feelings of how I would react if I had my desire granted right at that moment.

If it is something that would make me happy, then I feel the happiness at that moment. Remember, if you can cause yourself to become sad because of what you let yourself feel, then you also have the power to cause yourself to feel joy, happiness, excitement, enthusiasm and so on.

The next thing I do is believe it is real. Whatever I am visualizing and feeling, I allow myself to believe it is reality at that moment in time. Essentially, I see it, I feel it and I believe it is happening *now*. I don't worry about how it is going to materialize. That's God's job, and He is good at keeping His promises. See, this is my way of hoping for something that is not seen yet and hoping until it materializes. Anytime I start doubting, I ask God for forgiveness, because my Bible says in Hebrews 11:6, "Without faith, it is impossible to please God." I place the picture in my mind once again.

In the beginning this takes a lot of practice. But once you start seeing results, your faith builds even more. Sometimes I do not know the desires of my heart. That's when I visualize myself happy. I picture a smile on my face and feel the lightness in my heart. Then, it's just a matter of believing what I see and feel. Because God knows me so well, He knows just what it takes to make me happy, and extra happiness finds its way into my life. Oh, the evidence of things (previously) not seen!

Let me tell you about an instance when God honored my faith. Craig and I were still living in our two-bedroom house. The kids were growing, and the walls seemed to be closing in on us. Chloé was maturing and needed more and more privacy. I knew it was time to move to a bigger home, but our credit was a mess. In the early eighties, it was much harder to re-establish credit. Our jobs were still just jobs and not careers, so we were living pretty much from paycheck to paycheck. Thank God, it was much better than living from paycheck to *before* paycheck. Like my grandmother told me right after Craig and I wed, "Baby, if you know a check is coming, you can make things stretch until it comes."

Looking at the situation we were in, it seemed impossible to even hope for a new home. But I tell you, hope is what I did. When I went to bed at night, I closed my eyes and visualized my kids playing in a big, fenced backyard. I could feel the joy of seeing my kids happily playing in their own large backyard. I felt as though I was actually living that moment in time. I would also visualize walking through that house, calling the kids and Craig for dinner. I would even envision myself walking from one room to another, only to realize I had forgotten something in the other room. I could feel myself getting a little agitated because I knew I had to walk all the way back to the other room to get whatever I had forgotten. All the time I would say and believe, "This house is sooo big!"

Within a year of exercising my faith for a new home, Craig and I sold our two-bedroom, one-bath, gingerbread-style house near the freeway and moved into our new home. It sat on a greenbelt across the street from Five Mile Creek, and on the other side of the creek were the tennis courts and the city park with a two-mile walking trail. The area was very hilly and filled with beautiful large trees, flowers and small animals, and our home was in the middle of the block. We now had three bedrooms, two full baths, living room/dining room combination, den, kitchen with a breakfast bar, office, two-car garage and a big, fenced backyard. God is able!

Nothing had changed with us; we still had bad credit and we still had jobs and not careers. As a matter of fact, I did not return to college to finish up my Bachelor of Arts degree until after we were in our new home. But like I told you before, don't worry about how God is going to give you the substance of the things you hope for. That is His job. Your only job is to see it, feel it and believe it in that instant. God will cause people to come across your path or just give you a thought you never had before. New insight. New knowledge. You know what I mean?

There are so many ways God has brought to me the substance of things I hoped for. Our first year in the new house was pretty tight financially, but we pulled our purse strings and hung in there. We went the whole first year without den furniture, and we only had two bar stools. When we ate, the kids sat at the breakfast bar and Craig and I sat down beside them on the floor. When we were finally able to buy furniture, Craig's mother co-signed on the credit application for us. We purchased a sofa, love seat, cocktail table, four matching barstools and better mattresses and box springs for the kids' beds.

We lived in that house eleven years. There were many times when I would look out the atrium windows and see the kids playing in that big, fenced backyard. It was nothing for me to forget something and have to go all the way back down the hallway to get what I needed.

Speaking of faith, there is another prime example of living through faith in our lives. I remember one time, Craig wanted us to have some fun and go crawfishing as a family. I am not the outdoors type of person, but I figured, why not? So, we woke up before dawn that Saturday. We dressed in jeans with our socks pulled up over the leg of our pants. We also sported boots and long-sleeve shirts.

Girl, if you could have only seen us. We looked a mess! The four of us crowded into Craig's pickup truck, and off we went. On the way, I laid my head back and closed my eyes for a minute. During that minute, I visualized our fishing buckets filled with crawfish trying to climb over the top while the ones at the bottom were trying to pull them back down. Then I visualized us sitting around the dinner table laughing and talking with a big bowl of onion rice, steamed crawfish, salad and hot garlic bread.

By the time I finished seeing, feeling and believing, I was hungry. We even pulled out the sandwiches I had prepared for our trip. When we arrived at the water hole, it was still fairly dark. Craig baited our strings that were attached to a stick, and we sat around for about two hours. No crawfish! We even tried different areas around there to cast our strings, but still no crawfish! Not a one.

Craig became frustrated, packed the truck up and said, "Let's get out of here." I was a little disenchanted because by then I knew how faith worked, and I had made my desire known. I mean, I could even see myself mixing up that rice and pouring it into that bowl with the steam still rising.

We all got into the truck and headed for home. On the way, Craig said, "Wait a minute, just wait. I remember this place we used to go to and fish when I was a kid, and it's on the way home." I said, "Okay, let's go!"

We pulled up to that little piece of water, and there were people everywhere. Seeing all that activity seemed to put new life in us. Craig parked, and we all jumped out of the truck. Craig baited our strings again. Within two hours we left there with a whole mess of crawfish. We could have left sooner, but we were having such a wonderful time, we just did not want it to end. Now, I don't have to tell you what we had for dinner, do I? I was smiling from ear to ear.

When I am in the middle of my faith work, I don't share my vision with anyone – not even Craig. To me, it's something that is personal between God and me. Kind of like a pact. . . a "You do your part, and I'll do mine" kind of thing. When you pray for something, it is Jesus who helps you form the right image to get God's attention and achieve your desire.

Oh, let me tell you another story about faith. We still lived at Five Mile Parkway when our refrigerator stopped working. We didn't have a savings account then; we didn't think we could afford to save. I have since learned that, like with tithing, once you tuck your money away for savings, you don't really miss it at all. But, anyway, we did not have any money saved to speak of then, and we didn't know what we were going to do about getting another refrigerator. Craig had the refrigerator picked up for repairs, but we soon found out that the repairs were going to cost far more than the refrigerator was worth. So, there we were with this big hole in the kitchen where that icebox used to sit.

Now, I could have pondered on our lack of extra money or on the high price of refrigerators. But I did not. In my mind, there sat a shiny white refrigerator. And when I opened the door, it was full of food. I even pictured myself cleaning that refrigerator with a wet dishtowel. If you could have gotten inside my heart at that moment, you would have sworn I was enjoying a brand new appliance that I considered to be a blessing from God.

Well, two days later guess what was sitting in that hole? That's right – a brand new, shiny refrigerator. By that time, Craig had a good career going with a major corporation, so he decided to go to his credit union. I don't know what made him decide to try for a loan because we still had the bankruptcy on our credit report, and we sure didn't want to bother our parents for everything. But he went to the credit union anyway, and to our surprise, they gave him a signature loan. That was the first loan we had ever gotten on our own since the bankruptcy, and the credit union didn't even ask for collateral.

I never worried about how I was going to get my refrigerator. I just believed I already had it in my kitchen. It's amazing what can happen when you have faith.

Now, I have learned over the years how to be a working participant in this area and how to make my desires known to God. I'll tell you more about how you can impress upon your mind and heart the desires you wish to manifest. But first, I must tell you about a time back before I even knew how faith worked.

Girl, this was back during the roughest times Craig and I have known. I had just finished cooking breakfast one morning and was already wondering what we were going to have for lunch. I didn't want to concern Craig too quickly, but I had just cooked the last of everything. There was nothing in the freezer, nothing in the cabinets, and I had cooked the last of the eggs and Cream of Wheat.

I prayed. There was a peace inside that made me feel like everything would be okay, but we still did not have any food.

I finally told Craig about the dilemma. I know he could see the concern on my face but I also know he could feel the quietness of my spirit. As I explained the situation, he looked at me with a quiet, proud kind of love and said, "Baby, it's going to be all right. Wait here, I'll be right back." Craig left me in the kitchen and went into the bedroom. I could hear him rambling in the closet for a few minutes, and then he returned. He reached into his pocket and pulled out a $50 bill, put it in my hand and said, "I want you to take this and go and get what you can. I've been saving this $50 for a long time. You don't know how many times I almost pulled it out for us to spend."

With this said, I kissed him and hugged him, feeling my love and respect for him grow even stronger. To my surprise, I had tears of relief in my eyes. He looked at me and smiled. As he hugged me again, he said, "We are going to be all right. We are going to make it, Abby. Just hang in here with me, please."

Then, as he pulled away to look straight into my eyes again, he said, "I love you more than you will ever know, and together we can make it through any situation."

Now, girl! You're not gonna believe this one. There was another time we were out of food, and I didn't know what we were going to do for lunch. Nevertheless, I had such a peace inside. I just knew God was going to take care of the situation. Craig and I were reading the newspaper while the kids were playing in their room. That's when I came upon a full page advertisement. "Craig, listen to this." Then I read aloud, "Tent Sale. Name Brand Furniture for Less. Great Bargains. Come One, Come All to the Greatest Furniture Sale in Town." Now here's the good part, "Free Hot Dogs, Chips and Sodas." By the time those words crossed my lips, Craig was up helping the kids put on their coats. We went on down to that tent sale, had lunch and even brought some home for dinner!

Now, I had not mentioned to him that we were out of food, but Craig always knows what is going on in his house. He may have to wait for divine guidance to handle the situation, but he seems to always know the status. I think sometimes we as women think that men should have all the answers when, in fact, they are just as human as we are. That means, sometimes they don't know which way to turn either. And during those times, it's just best to be still. But when a man gets still and waits for divine guidance, women perceive it as a non-caring attitude.

I am glad that I learned early in our marriage that Craig really loves me and he really loves his family. I'm glad I learned that just because he is quiet sometimes doesn't mean he doesn't care. Most men try to solve more of their dilemmas from within; most don't have the need to voice everything like we do.

Just as my husband cares for his family, so does the Lord up above. Let me tell you, there was not one day or one mealtime through all those years that we went without eating. Now, I did not know about "faith work" then, but I did believe God would make a way, and that's what He did. He made a way out of no way, and He did just that over and over again.

Did you know trusting God and having faith grows with your experience? We have to understand that sometimes our desires are not God's desire for us, and we have to humble ourselves to the fact that He knows what is best for His children.

An Obedient Heart

The way my parents raised me helped prepare me to handle a very important fact of life – you don't always get what you want when you want it. They reared me by tilling the soil of my heart and making it right for sowing the seeds of patience, obedience and understanding.

When I was a teenager, my parents were not afraid to tell me no. "No, you can't go." "No, you can't have." "No."

My mother said that when she was growing up, her parents did not give her everything she wanted either. Her father often told her that if he said 'yes' to everything, she might not know how to accept 'no' when she became an adult. And life certainly does say 'no' sometimes.

"If my father had given me everything I wanted, your dad and I would probably not have made it through our first few years of marriage," Mom told me. "Those were tough times and I had to do without a lot of things. If I hadn't known how to accept that there were things I just could not have or buy right then, and had I not been willing to wait for things I wanted, I probably would have just walked right out of there."

One thing about it, I always knew that my parents loved me, and that helped ease the pain of being told 'no'. When I was in my early teens, I recall one day when my dad came into my room to have one of those talks. I was lying across my bed, and my father sat at the foot. After chitchatting a little, he said, "You know, you are really growing up fast. It seems like just yesterday you were a baby. I want you to understand that your mother and I love you more than anyone ever could, and we would never in our wildest dreams intentionally do or say anything that would cause you harm in any way."

I remember perking up a little as he said, "Abby, as you get older, there are going to be times when mama and daddy are going to have to use our judgement about certain things. And you may not understand why we don't let you go somewhere or do something that you want to do. You are going to have to trust that we love you and that our decisions have your best interest at heart." Looking back, he was right when he said, "You will not be able to say that about most people you are going to run into, but you will never have to worry if your mother and I are doing what is best for you."

Sure enough, later on in my teenage years, they had to make judgement calls that I did not understand at the time. And yes, they often hurt. But all in all, just like my father said, their decisions always were in my best interest over the long haul.

When the Bible commands us to "honor thy mother and thy father," I believe this is to prepare us for a relationship with God Himself. We should have a heart that submits to authority – His authority.

I used my parents' teachings to raise my own children. As an adult, I can still feel the effects of their lessons.

Here's a perfect example. Years ago, when Craig was in the midst of his career with IBM, I was in between jobs. I had just finished my B.A. degree, and I had this burning desire to work for IBM, also. The company had several "supplemental" positions available in their customer service department; "supplemental" meant these were three-month temporary positions. After three months in the position, the managers would make the decision whether to hire the individual or not. I decided it would be a good way for me to get my foot in the door, so I and about 10 or 15 others took the positions.

I worked hard. I wanted that job and the benefits. I also wanted the prestige that came when both husband and wife work for IBM. There really were a bunch of great workers in the running with me. We came up to the end of the three months and guess what? IBM had a company-wide hiring freeze. They could not hire any of us. Instead, the managers extended our contracts another three months. We were so grateful, so full of hope, and we worked even harder. By the time another three months rolled around, the hiring freeze still had not let up. We were all devastated, to say the least. Because of company rules or something, they could not extend our time. They had to let us all go, and that was certainly a sad, sad day.

Well, I found other things to do, including substitute teaching, but deep down, I really wanted to work for IBM.

About a year or so later, Craig heard that they were hiring in the customer service department again. I sent IBM an updated résumé and was granted an interview within the week. I thought the interview went well.

By then, the managers in this department were all different. In fact, some of the people who were on the phones taking customer service calls when I was there had become managers. The manager I interviewed with had already been informed of my prior performance. He was impressed, or so he said. Well, I waited to hear if I was going to get the job. I was confident. After all, I was already trained to fulfill the duties. Everything was stacked in my favor.

A week passed, but I didn't hear anything. I got anxious and decided to call the interviewing manager. "I'm sorry, Mrs. Smith, but the competition was stiff. We gave the job to another candidate. You should be receiving your letter in the mail soon." Needless to say, I was crushed. I hung up the telephone and cried like a little baby.

A few minutes later, Craig called. He was also shocked that I did not get the position. I know he hated to hear how broken I was, but I was so hurt! After I hung up with Craig, I laid back across the bed and cried. Yet from somewhere, I seemed to be comforted. "Lord, I know you know what's best for me," I prayed. "I don't understand what's happening right now, but I do know that you love me. Maybe you have a better job for me. I don't know; just please take care of me." Within a few more minutes, I was able to relax, nestled in a feeling of complete peace.

You know, God really does know what He is doing. I went on and became a certified special education teacher. Now I have a career with excellent retirement benefits. Plus, every holiday and vacation, I was off with the kids; they never had to come home to an empty house.

The pay in the public schools is not terrific, but the job itself is rewarding. I love helping children see their own self-worth. Some of my students come from broken homes. I try to make the seven hours a day that they are with me as positive, pleasurable and loving as possible. Special education or regular education, it does not matter. Kids respond to genuine love. They know when someone cares about them.

As it turns out, the cutbacks at IBM weren't over with yet. A couple of years ago, Craig took IBM's early leave package to avoid a possible layoff. While we anticipated that it might take a couple of months for Craig to find a new job, he was out of work for a year and a half. Instead of building a nest egg with his IBM leave package, we spent all of that money on day-to-day expenses during that dry spell.

Now, if I had gotten that job years earlier with IBM, I might have been out of work when he was, or at least worrying about if I would be the next one to go. But instead, my teaching job – my career – and God put food on the table and carried us through Craig's months of unemployment.

Working for IBM was the ultimate opportunity at one time to me. I never would have left that job to go into the teacher-training program that I did. And do you know what else? If special education had not been the only opening available in the program that year, I never would have gone into that particular field of education. That would have been a shame, because I absolutely love what I do.

There were many times during those 18 months that Craig heard me say, "Thank God, I didn't get that job!" So, you see? God knew. He knew what I had no way of knowing.

I certainly do believe that my mother and my father were responsible for helping me develop an obedient heart at an early age. That's what has kept me from being bitter when I don't get what I want. They taught me how to accept being told 'no'.

Trusting God

I learned another dimension to God's love when we trust Him while on vacation in Colorado Springs, Colorado. Our first trip there was such a beautiful experience. The snow-capped Rocky Mountains absolutely took our breath away. We had so much fun, and the highlight of our whole trip was the drive to the top of Pikes Peak.

We woke up early that morning to prepare for the trip to the top of the mountain, and Craig reminded us to bring along our coats and blankets. "It may be 75 degrees now, but as we climb that mountain, it's going to get colder and colder," he explained. Now, deep down, I didn't think Craig really knew what he was talking about. After all, this was his first time going to the top of a mountain, too. But, like we always try to do, we followed his advice.

We loaded our van down with blankets, pillows, coats, scarves, gloves and caps and then stopped at the neighborhood grocery store to buy some food for the trek. We were ready for our adventure. We checked in at the guard's desk at the Pikes Peak entrance where we were advised of the safety precautions and rules. After checking our brakes, we were given the clearance to go.

It was such a beautiful ride up. When we started out, Craig was driving, talking, laughing and looking around at all the beauty. But the further up that mountain we went, the quieter Craig became.

"Baby, are you all right?"

"Yeah, I'm just trying to pay attention to what I'm doing."

"But, baby, you're missing all the scenery. See, look at that! That's sooo beautiful."

"No, y'all go on and look. I've got to keep my eyes on the road. I'll look later."

"Okay, but you sure are missing a lot of beauty."

We kept going higher until we reached the halfway point. There was a rest area with restrooms and shops, so we got out and looked around, especially Craig. He had missed so much on the ride up. We pulled our hatch up on the van, and the four of us sat in the back with our feet dangling as we ate our lunch. It was so beautiful.

"Well, are we ready to finish this journey upward?" Craig asked. We all said, "Yes!" So off we were again. We went up, up, up. Now if you think Craig kept his eyes on the road before, let me tell you, that man didn't turn his head to the left or to the right for anything this time.

Finally, I said, "Craig, you have got to either slow down a lot or pull over and stop. Honey, you have to see this. It's too beautiful not to share."

He pulled over on the shoulder as far as he could and stopped. He looked all around, and his eyes lit up. "I have never in my whole life seen anything more beautiful," he said. It gave me so much joy to see him take it all in.

We jumped back in the van and continued going up, up, up Pikes Peak. Now, if you had been a fly on the windshield of that van, you would have laughed your wings off. Craig was still looking straight ahead, while I was looking around and hollering, "Oh, my goodness! Oh, my goodness!" Chloé's hands covered her face as she peeked between her fingers to view the awesomeness of the mountains. Meanwhile, Clayton was at the back of the van on the floor, praying and confessing all his sins from his earliest memories and promising never to do them again. By that time, Craig was laughing at all of us. I guess he looked out of the corner of his eye and used his rear view mirror to see that we all had on our coats, hats, gloves and scarves. On top of all that, we were all wrapped in our blankets. Well, Clayton was holding a tent meeting under his.

When we finally got to the top, we hurtled out of that van with such excitement. First it started snowing, and then the blizzard came. Yes, a blizzard! When a voice came over the loud speaker warning of an electrical storm, we hurried inside the souvenir shop for cover. We rested there a few hours while we waited for the snow to let up.

I'll never forget our experiences on Pikes Peak. When we finally made it back down to the foot of the mountain, it was 75 degrees and drizzling.

We went the whole year talking about our Colorado trip. There were times during the year when I would get to feeling down, and I would just think about the beauty of the Rocky Mountains. That alone would just lift my spirits. I figured, if God can do all that so majestically, then He can certainly take care of my little problems.

When it was time to plan our next vacation, we could not think of a trip without a stop in Colorado Springs. So, we decided to go from Dallas to Colorado Springs, from there to Aspen, then to Utah, on to Las Vegas, then to the Grand Canyon and finally back to Dallas.

That July day, we arrived in Colorado Springs, with even more excitement than we had the first time. Mind you, I always pray about our vacations before we leave. I pray that God will make it an enjoyable and exciting adventure.

After a day of sightseeing and lounging at the pool, we woke early the following day to prepare to hit the mountains. Craig did not have to tell us to get our coats and blankets this time, and he promised he would make an effort to look at the scenery.

As we approached the entrance to Pikes Peak, we noticed the long line of cars making U-turns; turning back, I guessed. When it was our turn at the gate, the guard told us that Pikes Peak was closed because of the annual Fourth of July race. Of course, that was the first time we heard of a race, and if we had known, we would have gone to our mountain the day before. Oh, I was so disappointed. We were deflated. Ordinarily, I would have tried to pump some life back into my family with a "Let's. . ." or "What about. . .?" But not this time. I just laid my head back on the headrest and closed my eyes.

I could feel my attitude turning negative and becoming out of control. Being in the middle of PMS did not help the situation one bit, if you know what I mean (and I know you do). Anyway, I didn't like my actions, and I sure didn't want to ruin our trip by being a sourpuss. I prayed, "Lord, help. I'm sorry for my behavior. I asked you to help us have a wonderful vacation and I know you will. Thank you." Right in there, right between me finishing my silent prayer and the peace from God returning to me, Craig said, "Baby, there are other mountains, we'll just have to find out how to get to them."

Vowing that we were going to make the best of our trip, we decided to head on to Aspen. But instead of going out the way we mapped, Craig gave in to his sense of adventure and decided to go by way of Independence Pass.

Within two hours, I was saying to Craig, "Can you believe all this beauty? Craig, if we had gone to Pikes Peak, imagine what we would have missed!" We were in a state of awe and my heart was praising God all the way. All I could say was, "Thank you, Lord."

Charting Your Path

Have you ever heard of mapping or blueprinting for life? Basically, it means establishing your desires for the upcoming years. I am sure that by now, you understand that you have to know what your desires are before you can see them, feel them and believe them.

At the first of every year, I do this thing called *mapping*, and it has been a tremendous blessing in my life. I sit in the middle of my den in front of the fireplace, and I have with me a blank, full-size photo album page – the kind with the peel-back plastic and sticky sheet. I also take a pair of scissors, a glue stick (just in case I need a little extra sticky stuff) and all of the magazines I can find in the house. Sometimes, I have to buy a few beforehand to add to the collection.

I ask God to guide me and inspire me as I make my desires known. I also ask Him to help me have the faith I need to see my desires materialize into the substance I hope for. I thank Him, and then I begin.

I always go through each one of my magazines searching, looking for pictures and words that represent my desires. And I always cut out the numerical year as large as I can find it and stick it at the very top of the page.

I remember the first time I did this. Included in the many desires I had posted all over my photobook page were a happy family, healthy looking hair, divine guidance, financial security, vacation getaways and inner beauty. Also represented were my desires to quit smoking and lose weight down to a healthy size.

To impress upon my mind the idea that I had quit smoking, I found an ad showing a cigarette between a woman's fingers. I cut that part of the picture out in the shape of a circle and stuck it to the page. Then, I cut out a thin strip, put glue on the back and placed it diagonally across the picture of the hand with the cigarette. In my mind, that image said, "No Smoking."

To impress my desire to lose weight and look good, I cut out the words "slim" and "sassy" and stuck them on the page. Beside these words, I put a small picture of women working out in a health club facility, exercise machines and all.

By the time I actually quit smoking, I had forgotten that it was among one of my goals for that year. When I do my mapping at the beginning of the year, I try to make a lasting impression in my mind with the pictures I choose. I always pray for guidance in this area because the better the impression, the easier it is to feel it. And if you can feel it, you can allow yourself to believe it. So, I make the best impression I can and go on.

I had tried for years to quit smoking. I called getting through the day on a pack and a half "cutting back." The biggest problem was that I really enjoyed smoking. Smoking was very relaxing, and I especially enjoyed the after-dinner smokes and smoking on long road trips. But I knew smoking was not a good habit to have. My kids were in elementary school, and they were learning about the hazards of smoking and pleading with me to stop. Craig had stopped cold turkey a few years earlier during a bout with the flu, and he never picked up another one again.

One time, I decided to take a carton of cigarettes, box and all, and put it on the barbecue grill. I thought, maybe if I burned the cigarettes on the grill, the smell would be so strong that it would make me sick from the fumes.

Well, I put the carton of cigarettes on the grill and started the fire. And guess what? The smell of all those cigarettes did make me nauseous. I made myself stand there in the midst of a hot Texas summer afternoon until the last piece of paper turned to ash. The smell was so strong, I vowed I would not touch another cigarette. That lasted until two o'clock the next morning.

Before the year I started mapping, every attempt I made at quitting smoking was futile. I just put the suggestion on my board and forgot about it. I did not worry about how it was going to happen and when, I just believed it would.

During that year, I was working on a temporary job when a friend of mine told me about a guy we worked with who had just been diagnosed with cancer. When the surgeon opened him up, he determined that the cancer was too bad and there was nothing he could do. The cancer had spread all over his body, so they just closed him back up. Now, let me tell you, that did something to me. I just kept seeing flashes of this guy chain-smoking like he always did.

I told Craig that I had to quit smoking, but I didn't know how. I had tried everything. He advised me to call a counselor. The counseling center told me that it had a one-week program that cost $400. I told her that the price was pretty steep and that I would have to talk it over with my husband. "Do it!" Craig said. "I'll check with our insurance and see if they will reimburse us."

I started the program on a Monday evening. The counselor told me over the phone to have my last cigarette the Sunday night before. When I arrived for my appointment, I had not had a cigarette all day and I was very apprehensive. I sat and talked with the counselor and told her how I had tried to quit so many times in the past. As I was still trying to make up my mind to go through the program, she looked at me and said, "If you still want a cigarette Friday, I'll give you your money back." And with that, I said, "Okay, you've got a deal."

I started the program right then. She took me into a small room with individual cubbyholes. I sat down at one of the stalls. All that was there was this big ashtray, a waste can and a big cut out picture of a diseased lung.

There were ashes and cigarette butts everywhere... the desk, the floor, the waste can, the ashtray. Everywhere! The counselor explained all the rules, "During this week, the only time you can smoke is in this room. Don't wash your hair or your outer clothing this week. Just put your clothing in a pile in your closet each evening until this week is up."

After those instructions, she laid a carton of my brand of cigarettes in front of me. Then, she put a little box shaped device on my right hand. She explained that every time I raised my arm to smoke a cigarette, it would give a little shock that was more of an annoyance than anything else.

The counselor opened the carton of cigarettes and took out a pack. She opened the pack, gave me one and told me to light it without inhaling. She told me to smoke it all the way down to the filter, taking short puffs, being careful not to inhale, and then blowing the smoke out. The object was to try to get through that whole carton in one session, which caused rapid movement of my arms, which caused that box to shock me every second to the point of utter annoyance.

I did that every evening for five days. On the third day, I was shown a tape about emphysema, which is what my grandfather died from a few years earlier. The counselor also told me that the cigarette ads often times show beautiful women, but they never show the beautiful woman with a cigarette in her mouth. They know that smoking does not make a woman look beautiful. That was something that really hit home. After all, that was the reason I started smoking. I started smoking at age 16 because I thought it would make me look sophisticated, beautiful and cool – just like the women in the ads. But my counselor was right. I have yet to see a cigarette ad with the cigarette in the woman's mouth.

My counselor told me that once the week was over, if I never gave in to smoking that first cigarette, I would never smoke again. I tell you, after enduring those daily smoke sessions, smelling smoke in my clothes every time I walked into my closet and learning it was okay not knowing what to do with my hands without a cigarette stuck in them, I did not want to see, taste nor smell another cigarette, ever.

The thought of smoking today, well over ten years later, causes me to have a slight cough. It's a reminder that smoking is not for me.

Would you believe that in that year of mapping, I quit smoking and I was on my way to losing 65 pounds? I sure was.

Earlier that year, I was getting dressed to go shopping and discovered that I could not tie up my tennis shoes. I was so embarrassed, but I asked Craig to tie them up for me. By the time he finished, tears were running down my cheeks. I had not realized that I had gotten that big. Craig hugged me and said, "I love you just the way you are, but I want you to be happy. I can't stand it when you are unhappy no matter what the reason."

I started a reputable diet program that following Monday. It took me a year and a half to lose 65 pounds, but it was a healthy choice. The one thing that really helped me lose weight over such a long period of time was keeping a personal diary. I took that diary everywhere, and I used it as therapy. The hardest times for me were weekends when I was out and about with my family.

I remember one time we were out when Craig stopped at a gas station and asked if we wanted anything to snack on. I said, "No," but the kids said, "I do! I do!" Craig came back with Cheetos. When I heard the bags opening and smelled the aroma of those chips, I grabbed my diary, and wrote, "Dear God, they are back there with those Cheetos. Please, please, help me to be strong. I know I am learning how to eat properly, and my weight is coming off slowly, which means I will keep it off. Please Lord, help me not to give in to temptation. Don't let me turn around and take those chips." I would just write and write until I convinced myself and the urge to cheat passed. That really worked for me.

A few years later, a lady who was a long-term substitute teacher in the classroom right next to me became a good friend. She was going through a very difficult time in her life. A former friend had taken her husband, leaving her and her small son to fend for themselves. After being divorced for a year, she was still bitter and did not know how to get her life back on track. She was always in church. . . always. Nevertheless, she was still searching for something. searching for happiness.

I started sharing with her about mapping and building her future at that moment in time. I tried to explain how to have faith in things that are good and stop holding on to all the bad things in her past. She became very interested in mapping and asked me a lot of questions about how to map for herself. I told her I would show her my board, which is something I had never done before, being the private person that I am. But I was compelled to share my desires with her and show her how to map out her own desires. Actually, through the process of mapping, you realize sometimes for the first time what your desires really are.

The next day, I took my mapping page to school with me, and I told my friend we could talk about it during lunch.

During my planning period, Craig showed up in the doorway of my classroom. Girl, he looked so good. Unfortunately, he was getting ready to catch an airplane to California, and I always get sad when he leaves. Craig came to say goodbye and tell me that he would phone every chance he could. He's always so good about that.

While Craig was there, I introduced him to my friend. After he left, she said, "Wow, he's handsome." Pooching out my bottom lip to pout, I explained that he was on his way out of town. "Poor baby," she said. "He'll be back."

We joined up later in my classroom to discuss mapping. She was really going through a difficult time in her life. And being the single parent of a little boy, she longed to be married again. Sometimes she got depressed, because she felt undesirable even though she was a pretty woman. Her self-esteem was so low.

I talked to her about imaging before we got to the subject of mapping. "Close your eyes and think of your wedding day," I told her. She closed her eyes. "Visualize yourself in your wedding dress walking down that aisle, thanking God for the person He sent into your life. Walk down that aisle knowing in your heart you have made the right choice."

I warned her against putting a face on her groom. "Let God bring the right man to you," I said. "Don't worry about how or when. Just know that He will give you the desires of your heart. Every time you start to doubt that you will get married again, just visualize your wedding again and feel all of the emotions. Believe it's real." She opened her eyes and smiled like she felt full of hope. I couldn't help but smile back.

On top of feeling lonely, she was making decisions about daycare centers and schooling for her son. I told her, "Every time you have to make a difficult decision, pray about it first. Then imagine how you would feel making the right decision. Imagine how grateful and thankful you would feel as everything worked out for the best," I told her. "Now, believe you are experiencing that right now, and you will be led down the right path." I reminded her that God is not the author of confusion.

Finally, I pulled out my mapping and explained how it worked so she could do one of her own. We talked about what each image represented. Then she noticed the picture of a Volvo 240 on the left side of the page. I told her that I had cut that picture out of the newspaper and colored it red myself. She looked at me kind of puzzled and said, "You drive a red Volvo 240, don't you?"

"I do now, but when I placed that picture on the page at the beginning of the year, I didn't know how we would be able to own one. I just believed we would." She just grinned.

It was turning out to be an enjoyable lunch period. We went on down the page as it showed my desire to travel. I had little pictures of airline tickets cut out of a magazine, an airplane tilted up like it was taking off and a picture of two people walking by the ocean. That's when I became very quiet, and my eyes moved from the travel scenes to the lower right side of the page. I could not believe my eyes! I had a picture of a stack of money beside the words, "IBM Club." Tears rolled, and I mean rolled, down my cheeks.

"What is it?" she asked.

With tears still streaming down, I said, "This is where Craig is going. He's on his way to the club today. Right now!"

I explained to her that Craig was in marketing, and the IBM Club was IBM's way of rewarding their top performers for the year. It was Craig's first year in marketing, and putting the IBM Club on my mapping page was a long shot. She looked at me and said, "Aren't you glad you did?"

I looked at her again and she said, "What?"

"In three days I'll be meeting Craig in Los Angeles, and from there, we're going to fly to Hawaii for five days and four nights. It is going to be a honeymoon for us, since we never had one before."

She looked back at my mapping page and before I knew it, we were both standing there with tears in our eyes. Actually, by then, I was pacing back and forth with my arms stretched towards heaven, thanking God for my many blessings.

As our lunch period came to a close, she hugged me and said, "You are sooo blessed. You don't know how much you have helped me." From that point on, we became very good friends. We talked about anything and everything while she was on her long-term substitute assignment.

P a r e n t i n g

One day we got on the subject of raising children. She loved her little boy, and she wanted the best for him. I cautioned her about trying to be his best friend. "He will have plenty of friends, but he needs you to be his mother. You're the one person he can look up to and depend on to tell him what is right."

Her son had been misbehaving since his father left. He was only two or three at the time. We talked about setting up a reward and consequences program with her son. I told her the main thing was that she stay in control of her household, being firm yet fair with her son. I told her that Craig and I have never looked at our two children as cute little dolls. We have always looked at them as two people we are responsible for preparing to live productively in this world. We take parenthood just as seriously as our marriage. We are strict, firm but fair parents, and our kids know they are loved. They know that our family takes priority in our lives.

And we try our best to walk right before them – to be good examples. We use our marriage and our family life as a classroom for our kids to learn how to treat their future husband, wife and children. We model respect and open communication. We are their example, and we don't take that lightly.

With our kids, Craig and I always try to show a united force. If we have a disagreement about how to handle one of the kids, we discuss the point out of their hearing range. Some of our biggest disagreements have been over the kids and how they should be raised. Being two different people with two different opinions makes that natural, but we do respect each other's right to have an opinion. Ultimately, we know that each of us only wants the best for our children.

When our kids were teenagers, it was a challenge. I would not – could not – have done it without divine intervention. Anytime a situation came up, even everyday stuff, I asked God to give me guidance. I believed He would answer, and sure enough, He revealed what to say or do. My job then became putting the revelation into action. Then, when I said or did what was revealed to me and it turned out right (and it always did), the only one I could thank for it was God.

In order to be effective parents, you have to be consistent and have rules that are enforced. Kids need to grow up in an environment with structure and boundaries. As they grow and learn the importance of rules and self-control, the parents have to learn to let go.

We have to start slowly letting go, even while they are still at home. They need opportunities to test their wings before they leave the nest. They need to see for themselves that they can make good decisions. Letting go slowly while they are still at home builds their confidence.

So many kids, especially boys, start getting into trouble the closer they get to finishing high school. They are scared. After all, they are old enough to see that a lot of people aren't doing so well in the world. Some are on welfare, some on the streets, some steal to make a living. They see all of this, and they just get plain scared. They wonder how they will make a living. how they will get a nice house, a nice car and nice clothes. They wonder how they will get the things that their parents have provided for them.

Rather than look like a personal failure, it soothes their hearts to blame their failure on drugs, alcohol or what have you. We need to let our kids know that we don't expect them to be able to afford all of the things that they have been accustomed to right off the bat. Parents should share some of their personal experiences about when they first left home and were on their own. It lets kids know that it is probably not going to be easy starting out, but they too can make it in this world.

When you start letting go slowly while they are still home, kids do learn to trust their own decisions more. It really is a long process. One of the ways I started letting go of Chloé was to stop asking about her homework. Now mind you, I was still asking

Clayton and checking his homework because he is three years younger. When I first started letting go, Chloé's grades dropped. But instead of panicking and checking her homework again, I let her face the consequences. The consequences were losing phone and TV privileges for a couple of weeks. And when I said two weeks, that is what I meant. After this, her grades would always improve without my help. This process was building her self-confidence.

When things suddenly change in the household, it is wise to inform the kids. When I started my "hands-off" strategy, I noticed that Chloé seemed sad and was trying to get some attention. I realized what was going on, so I sat her down and we had a talk. I told her I was giving her the room she needed to grow into a responsible adult. "It's hard for a parent to step back and watch their children make mistakes. But you need room to make your own decisions, even if that means that you mess up sometimes. You need room to make mistakes while you are still at home." After our conversation, Chloé's attitude and behavior seemed to return to normal. One thing did change, though. She was more confident than ever.

I have always used different situations and tragedies in our life to teach our children many lessons. Two instances come to mind, and both happened during the kids' elementary years.

Craig was out of town on business and it was Fair Day. That was the first year Craig and I did not take the kids to the fair together, even though the State Fair of Texas was an event that we looked forward to each year. We missed him, but I was determined to make it an enjoyable day for them.

We left early that Saturday morning, and they were so excited. When we arrived, I showed them exactly where we would meet if we happened to get separated in the crowd, but our intentions were to stay together. We walked around, played games and visited some of the attractions for a few hours.

After a while, I pulled the kids to the side and gave them each $20. "When this money is gone, it will be time to go home," I told them. They were both looking at me with a kind of wide-eyed wonderment. We walked over to the ticket counter to exchange their money for two coupon books each.

"We are going to stick together," I instructed. "We will go with one person to the ride they choose, and then we will go with the other person to the ride they choose." So, that's what we did. We took turns back and forth for the next couple of hours. For some reason, they did not make snappy decisions. Instead, they went around the fair choosing how they were going to spend their money, and I just followed along in amazement.

But I tell you, what really made my heart sing was when they were each down to their last two coupons. They stood there in the middle of the fairground trying to decide how to have their last bit of fun. About that time, Clayton said, "Chloé, how about if we put our tickets together and buy something to eat?" They looked up at me for approval, and I said, "Don't look at me. That's your money!" They smiled, and we were off to the concession stand. After deciding on a large order of fries and a foot-long chili cheese dog, we were on our way home.

The kids sat in the back seat vowing to split everything equally once we got home. When we pulled into the garage late that afternoon, the two jumped out of the car and ran into the house, leaving me to fend for myself. All of a sudden, I heard Chloé screaming, "Mama! Mama, our TV is gone!" I ran into the house and stood in the middle of the den. Sure enough, the TV was gone, and things were in total disarray. Someone had stolen our TV, stereo, money, jewelry. . . the works.

After calling the police and making a crime report, it took hours to straighten everything out. I was surprisingly calm about the situation, given that Craig was a thousand miles away.

After I finished cleaning up, I sat the kids down for a talk. I could tell they were still feeling insecure and unsafe in their own home. I shared a little of those feelings, too. I talked to them about morals, self-reliance and doing unto others as they would want others to do unto them. When I finished, I looked around the room and then said, “I know you don’t feel safe right now, but you are. The officers helped me secure all the windows again. We’re safe, okay?

Chloé looked at me and said, “Mama, can we go spend the night at Nana’s?”

Although the idea sounded pretty good to me, I told them, “We will be all right. This is our house, and this is the situation we are in. We have taken care of the problem, and there’s no need to alarm Nana. She would worry about us needlessly. Plus, your daddy will be home tomorrow evening.”

Then I told them when it is right to call family. “Now sweetheart, if we were in any danger, like not being able to close the doors, we would go to Nana’s. Anytime you are in real danger, don’t hesitate to call your relatives because you are blessed with a lot of them that love you, but if you can take care of the situation yourself, do that.”

We spent a quiet evening at home. The kids ended up in my room with their sleeping bags. We ate popcorn and read stories before saying our bedtime prayer, kissing each other goodnight and falling off to sleep.

Learning about Life through Death

On down life’s road, we had a death in our family that shook us to our very core. Lolo, Craig’s grandmother, died of colon cancer. She was like a second mother to him. She had such a sweet and gentle spirit, and I just wanted to bask in her love forever.

Chloé was her first great grandchild, and Clayton was her first great grandboy. She loved those two with all her heart, and they dearly loved her. She would take them shopping downtown with her. They would ride the city bus, which the kids loved to do. Oh, she was special to them, to me, to us.

The two of us enjoyed going to musicals together, but then again, I always enjoyed her company. Craig was her first grandson, and he and his mother lived with Lolo while his mother finished high school and college. Lolo showered Craig with so much love and a great deal of patience.

Watching Lolo shrivel up and die from colon cancer over that year was indescribable – agonizingly painful. After her funeral, we were all in misery for days. . . months. . . no, years. I told the kids, "Time is the only thing that heals matters of the heart."

I wanted so badly to pretend that Lolo was just on vacation or just gone away for a while. But I knew that would not be healthy mentally. I knew I had to deal with her death in a more permanent way. I felt so lonely. . . empty. Oh, my God! It was sooo painful. It hurt so, so, so bad.

Every night during my bath, I would force myself to acknowledge that Lolo was dead and not coming back again. I would lie back in that tub and ask God for help, and I would just cry and cry and cry. And then one day, I realized that it did not hurt as bad. And along with that thought came a bittersweet feeling. I was thankful to God that the hurt was getting less intense, but then I cried because I was afraid that I was beginning to forget her, and she was too dear to me for that to happen. I did not ever want to forget her, but as time passed, it all worked out. The pain is gone, but the memories are sweet; they are so sweet.

A few years later, I was talking to the kids about relationships. Chloé was a pre-teen at the time. I told her that pretty soon she would be dating. Of course, she looked forward to that.

"As you two get older, you will have to realize that there are going to be good days and bad days," I told her. "Sometimes the bad days can turn into bad months and even into a bad year, but you have to keep a positive attitude and understand that bad times are only temporary."

With a very serious tone in the air, I explained, "There are a lot of teens, and adults, who kill themselves because they don't think their situations could get better. And when you start dating, a courtship may run into problems, and the relationship may end. If it is someone you really care for, that can be very painful."

I reminded them, "Do you remember how much your heart hurt when Lolo died?"

They both looked at me and gave a quiet, "Yes."

"You didn't think the pain would stop, did you?"

They looked kind of sad as they both said, "No."

"Does it still hurt like it did?"

They looked at me a minute, and I could almost see the revelation in their eyes as they quietly said, "No."

"Why do you think that is?"

Chloé said, "Because time has healed us."

I could see their eyes get a little misty as I continued by telling them, "And just like time healed that hurt, time will heal heartaches. Just have faith that it will be all right and don't give in to the fear of pain. The pain will help you to grow as you trust in God."

Now I tell you what, years later both of those kids made it through their first courtship heartaches like troopers. Even though they were hurting, they continued to march to the drumbeat of their own lives. I try to teach my kids not to hide from their own emotions. Instead, they deal directly with their true feelings.

The other day, Craig and I were riding along in the van when all of a sudden he said, "Abby, I've been thinking. I don't know why this came to mind, but if I die before you, I hope you will give away all of my things and even buy a new bedroom set and just start over."

I said, "Honey, I know I will handle it the best way I can. I know from experience that with God's help, I will address the situation and deal with it."

He smiled and said, "I know you will."

Organization

Being a co-parent in our household with teenagers was sometimes a difficult job, especially since I was a working mother, also.

Without my planner, I would be lost. I carry my weekly planner with me everywhere. The two things I do religiously once a year are mapping at the beginning of the year and buying a new planner the last week of the year. After I purchase my planner, I use the last week of the year to go through my planner and write down all the birthdays of family and friends. I write in our anniversary and any standing appointments that are already scheduled. I use the school calendar to write in all the vacation days, days the report cards are issued, the beginning and ending of each six-week school term and all paydays.

Back then, if I had to put one or both of the kids on punishment, I would note the day it would end. If I asked the kids to read a book by a certain time, I would write that in my planner. I recorded all of their appointments to keep myself informed of their activities.

I keep track of the beginning and ending of all of Craig's business trips, remind myself to drop off or pick up our cleaning, make important phone calls and plan my weekly menu. I use my planner for everything. I record all my meetings, both personal and business. This is how I keep up with my salon and nail appointments. It's my reminder to pick up my herbs and what have you from the health food store.

Keeping a planner is true freedom. You don't have to try to remember all of that information in your head, and it actually frees your mind from overload. The only two things you have to remember to do are to write everything down and to look at that day's notes.

I remember the day Chloé said, "Mama, get your book because I have some dates for you." I got my planner and sat down.

As she flipped through her planner, she said, "Okay, January 18th, present award to the mayor from our Dallas County Community College's Leadership Conference; February 17th, senior pictures; March 1st, 2nd and 3rd, Zeno Conference in Lawton, Oklahoma; and May 20th, graduation day!" As I wrote the dates down, I wondered how I could be happy and sad at the same time? My firstborn was graduating from high school. I could only hope that we had prepared her for life as an adult.

My daily prayer has been, from the time they were babies, "Lord, please raise Chloé and Clayton through Craig and me." I would and still do say, "Give us what to say and how to say it, what to do and how to do it. Father, you know them, you made them. Please raise them through us. Amen." I cannot take any of the credit for how they have turned out. I asked for help and received it from the beginning.

More Parenting

Since I don't have any brothers, I have relied heavily on Craig when it comes to raising Clayton. I never heard my father tell a son what he should and should not do. For instance, one day Clayton had a soccer game, and it was raining. I was not going to take him until Craig called from out of town and said, "Baby, he's a boy. Take him on, and he'll be all right." I took him, wondering all the way how Craig knew just when to call.

I later found out that Clayton had gone to the phone in the other room and called his daddy, leaving a message at his office saying, "Daddy, help! Mama won't take me to my game just because it's raining. Call her, please. I've got to be there! I can't miss this game, Dad!"

As we pulled into the parking lot by the soccer field, a big bolt of lightning lit up the sky. Clayton looked at me and said, "Now Mom, rain is one thing. I can play in the rain, but lightning is dangerous. I can't play in this, so let's go back home." So, I followed my little man's advice, and we went home.

There have been many instances where I know I would have made a certain decision if I had been a single parent of a male child. There have been many times Craig has had to shed light from a male perspective on a given situation.

Men and women really do see things differently. But I have made sure that both my son and my daughter know how to wash dishes, mow the yard, fold clothes, take out the trash, clean their rooms, change a tire, mop or vacuum the floors and other chores that help kids feel needed and responsible.

Speaking of feeling needed, I required our kids to do volunteer work in the community for two consecutive summers before they could work for pay. Now, when I first told them that they would have to volunteer, they didn't like it one bit. But I stood my ground, and I'm glad I did. In one of Chloé's first semester senior essays, she told of how she initially did not understand why I would make her volunteer instead of making money. But in her essay, she also said, "Now, I am glad she did. Because of volunteering, I feel needed in the world, and that feeling has helped me to grow into the confident person I am today."

Standing your ground; that is the toughest part of being the parent of teenagers. Knowing when to bend the rules and how far is a dilemma Craig and I have found ourselves in time after time. All I can say is, "By the grace of God." But, all in all, Craig and I enjoy our kids and what they bring to our lives. They keep us young, because we refuse to allow them to make us old. We always find time for each other.

Time for Us

Craig and I dropped the kids off at two different functions one night, and we had about three and a half hours to spend before picking them up. We went to the bookstore and picked out a couple of interesting books. After leaving the bookstore, we went to a nice restaurant where we sat and talked for awhile. Then Craig asked to see my book. He started reading the introduction while I looked through his magazine. He said, "This is interesting, listen to this." And he read a paragraph to me. I took the book and he took his magazine and we sat there reading shoulder-to-shoulder until our meal was served.

As we left the restaurant arm in arm, I asked Craig, "What are we going to do when the kids grow up and leave?" We stopped at the van door, he kissed me and then looked me right in my eyes and said, "We're going to do more of what we did tonight – enjoy life."

The one thing I never wanted to happen was for the kids to finally leave home and Craig and I find ourselves trying to get reacquainted. So, along the way, I made it my business to continue to court my husband and keep our love alive. I'll tell you more about that, too. . . later.

Part 3

More Ties that Bind

A Home Built by Faith

When Craig first started talking about building a new home, I was totally against the idea. I had heard horror stories about people losing money or being disappointed by the finished product. If we were going to move again, I wanted to purchase an existing home. I just did not want the hassle. Craig dropped the subject of building for a few months, but then he brought the matter up again. After a while, I agreed on the condition that he would take care of everything and stay on top of the project every step of the way.

When we finally picked out our lot and broke ground, we were so excited! Every evening after work, we jumped in the van to go see what the construction crew did that day. Of course, Craig made several visits to the site each and every day. Craig certainly kept his promise. In fact, it became a standing joke about him always being at the site annoying the workers.

As the months dragged on, the house was taking shape. Before long, we entered the stage of building when I had to make a lot of the aesthetic decisions like types of carpet, tile, wallpaper. . . all of that stuff.

Actually, the building job and selling our house on Five Mile Parkway was going great. Craig had a few run-ins with the builder, but nothing out of the ordinary. Just as he told me he would, Craig stayed on top of everything. . . or so we thought.

One evening after the electricity was working, Craig brought me to the site. We took pictures and goofed around for a long time since we had lighting even after dark. At that point, the carpet and tile had not been laid yet. The wallpaper and painting still had to be done. Mirrors needed to be selected and installed. Actually, there was still a lot that had to be done – kitchen cabinets, molding, the front walkway, sidewalk, mailbox, fireplace, landscape and a lot of little nit-picky things – before we could close on our new home.

The next day during my planning period at school, I was checking my voice messages, and there was a message from Craig. Before I finished listening, my mouth was standing wide open.

When Trouble Comes

"Baby, listen. I've got something to tell you. The manager at the lighting store had his guys take down all the light fixtures from the house." All I could think of were those big glass fixtures that took me over three hours to select.

"Oh, why?" I heard myself say into the telephone receiver.

The message continued, "I jumped back in my car and rushed over to the construction office. Baby, they are gone! I looked in the window, and the desks, chairs, file cabinets – everything is gone!"

Sounding heartbroken, Craig said, "I am so sorry I have to tell you this on the telephone, but I did not want you to hear about it anywhere else. Listen, baby, try not to worry, and I'll do my best to take care of everything."

Well, the builder had filed bankruptcy and taken off in the night, leaving five houses under construction. As it turned out, my husband finished our house. He became the builder and the foreman, contracting out each job himself. I love that man!

There was a time when I was afraid that maybe we wouldn't be able to finish the house. Craig was having problems with the city inspector, and the buyer for the house on Five Mile Parkway backed out of the contract at the last minute. Getting the final loan approval was no picnic either. I started falling back on an old habit – worrying. But it seemed like the more I worried, the worse the situation became and the more frustrated Craig became. One day, I pulled myself together, said a prayer and did my part in bringing closure to the purchase of our house. I imagined myself walking on the Berber carpet of our new home. In my mind, I had on my bathrobe and house shoes, and I went over to my leather sofa and sat down. I believed it with my heart, and I thanked God in advance for blessing us with a new home. I kept that vision in my mind until the day we sold our house and closed the loan for the new one. I just stepped from the hope for the thing not seen into the evidence of that which was (previously) not seen.

About three months after we moved in, I was walking through our new home in my bathrobe and house shoes, and I went over to the sofa and sat down. When I realized I was living my vision just as I had imagined it three months earlier. . . yeah, you got it! I cried and cried and thanked God for His blessings.

It took Craig and me approximately 18 months to get over the emotional effects of being left with the total responsibility of finishing our home. The builder had received money from the bank to pay the contractors, and Craig had signed off on the agreements stating that the work was complete. In seven or eight of the cases, the contractor never received the money that the bank gave the builder on their behalf. Meanwhile, some of the contractors were honest and told us that they had already been paid for their work. We questioned the others, but we could never prove if they had been paid or not. So, on some parts of our home, I'm sure we paid the contractors twice. For a long time, Craig said he would never build again.

In my husband's defense, I can say that he looked for a builder for over two years before he decided to go with this one. And then, it took him six months to sign on the dotted line.

After the construction company ran off and we had to go to the different suppliers, they were still in shock. Everywhere we went, the owners and sales people would tell us that Dan had been in the business for over ten years, and he was the last person they would have ever thought to do such a thing.

Now he says, "If we build again, I know what to look for." He told me that he would have written in the contract that our builder would have a special account for our construction only. The money for our site would not be mixed in with the money for any other sites. He said he would get a list of the contractors and a list of all the suppliers, and that he would sign off on each draw personally. In addition, he would also contact the contractors and suppliers to make sure they were paid. And of course, he said he would still visit the site as regularly as he did.

I learned a valuable lesson. I learned not to dwell on fears. My fears were strong enough in me to bring to me what I feared, just as my hopes can be strong enough in me to bring to me what I have hoped for. Yes, it was a very difficult time for us, but we made it through.

Expressing Love

I bet you can't guess who I ran into downtown while I was at the County Records Building getting copies of our deed to close the sale on Five Mile Parkway. It was my friend – the substitute teacher. She just hugged me and she was so bubbly.

"Abby! I'm getting married, and this is my fiancé." He was tall and very good-looking, and she looked so pretty and so happy.

"Everything you told me was right," she said. "Thank you so much. We are in a hurry. We came down here to get our marriage license, but I'll call you later," she yelled as the elevator door closed.

Isn't God good? Faith.

Seeing my friend reminded me of how much God had blessed me with my wonderful husband. I decided to do something special for Craig to thank him for his hard work in finishing our home. I decided to have a painting done to christen our home and to say, "Thank you."

Craig and I grew up on the same street with a friend who is now an artist in Dallas. Elwood had already done a sketch of me for our bedroom, so I called him up with another project.

"Elwood, I need your help. Can you do a 72-inch by 42-inch canvas sketch for my den?"

"Well, what did you have in mind?"

"We have a photo of Craig's side of the family," I said.

"How many subjects are we talking about?"

"Thirteen," I said.

"Well, do you have any idea about what you want? Black and white or color?"

"Well, I like the sketch you did of me in black and white with splashes of color on my dress."

"Oh, yeah! Okay, I'll see what I can do."

"Now listen, don't you dare breathe a word of this to Craig. I want it to be a surprise!"

I took Elwood the photo, and what he came up with is so beautiful. The picture was all done in charcoal and colored pencils. I presented it to Craig and thanked him for all the trouble he had gone through to get our house built. He was so pleased with the gift.

Coping with PMS

I quit drinking coffee years ago when I realized how bad it was affecting my moods during PMS. Sinus pressure, headaches, complete exhaustion, temper outbursts, extreme mood swings, irritability, restless sleep, depression, nervousness, indecisiveness, confusion, memory loss, weight gain and sore breasts are symptoms I remember. That's right. For 14 days out of every month, I was miserable and hard to live with. I had read that chocolate and caffeine are bad for PMS sufferers.

After sitting in my closet crying uncontrollably for two straight hours only a few hours after eating a chocolate candy bar, I knew right then I had to choose: the chocolate or my marriage. From that moment on, chocolate has not passed through my lips; that has been over 17 years. There are other foods that affect my PMS, also. Everybody is different. For me, chocolate is by far the worst. Next would be caffeine, sugar, white flour and then salt. I know that sounds like everything, but it's not.

During PMS, I eat a lot of vegetables and grilled or baked fish and chicken. I eat fruits, but not a whole lot. Sometimes the natural sugar in some fruits causes me to feel bad. When I don't eat chocolate, caffeine, white flour, sugar and salt on those days, I really do feel more balanced and in control.

Chloé has the same problems with chocolate; it causes her to have angry outbursts. She hasn't had chocolate in a long time. However, she does still eat other sweets, but they don't cause her to feel as bad. She just has more self-control when she has not had chocolate.

I know a lot of women who have problems with their teenage daughters. Or should I say that they give each other problems? I think that's more like the truth. It is hard enough to keep yourself in check during PMS, let alone two people in the same household with PMS at the same time. It's not easy.

Chloé and I both took herbal supplements to balance our hormones and "tame the spirits" each month. We both kept up with the days in our planners. We could all tell when Chloé had forgotten to take her herbs. She didn't feel well, and it showed all over her face and in her attitude and behavior. Five minutes after she took the vitamins and herbs, you could definitely tell a big difference. But the combination Chloé used did not work well for me. Everyone's body chemistry is different, you know?

There are many herbs and herbal combinations at the health food stores that help with PMS and menopause, as well. When I have a hard time sleeping, which I normally do during PMS, I will use herbs because they are natural. Herbs are God's food and medicine for the body He created.

Maintaining a moderate exercise program has helped ease PMS symptoms for me, as well. I walk for 45 minutes a day, four days a week. Exercising gives me more energy and it is a great benefit for my sex life.

And PMS can really cause a serious situation in a marriage. It can pull couples apart because of the symptoms that arise from raging hormones. I have found that eating properly, taking vitamins and herbs and regular exercise have greatly controlled the symptoms each month.

Who Are You?

Girlfriend, don't forget to keep growing spiritually and developing your hobbies and interests, even after you are married. Besides being someone's mother or someone's wife, you are who you are spiritually, and your interests, hobbies and beliefs make up the uniqueness in you.

Second only to my spiritual growth, my marriage has top priority in my life. But my marriage is not my life. My marriage is not who I am.

Don't ever lose you. Nurture you. Pamper you. Continue to improve you. Don't ever stop growing.

Now, this may sound selfish to you, but I love me. God made me just like He made Craig. He made me just like He made Chloé. He made me just like He made Clayton. He loves each one of them, and He loves me. It would be wrong of me to put more importance on their lives than I put on my own.

When you love yourself, you should value yourself, your interests and your hobbies. Then, you learn to enjoy you and what you are all about. When you can enjoy yourself, others can enjoy you also.

In my relationship with Craig, I still make time for myself. I love to read, so I read. One of my interests is natural healing, so I make time to learn all about it by reading, talking to people, visiting the health food store and trying different herbs. I develop my interests.

And my hobby is raising AKC Toy Chihuahuas, so that's what I do. I don't put my personal growth on the back burner for my family or anyone else. I incorporate my interests with theirs. No one gets lost in the shuffle. Everyone in our family is important, and each of us knows that.

Stand Up for You

Do we argue? Of course we do! Craig and I are two different people with ideas that sometimes conflict. But I can give us this much – we don't argue as much as we used to. Actually, it's very seldom these days, nothing like it used to be.

I remember one time back when we were in business that Craig and I got into a big argument. He was feeling his man-size entrepreneurial oats. I can't remember what we were arguing about, and I don't know what got into him. All I remember is that he told me I had to do something because he said so. That right there took the situation from bad to worse. I looked upside that man's head, and of course, by then I was cross-eyed.

"Craig Smith, as long as you live and call yourself my husband, don't you ever fix your mouth to tell me what I have to do!" I told him, "True enough, the Bible tells me to submit unto my husband, but that is the choice I make. I make the choice whether I want to submit to you or not. You can't make me do anything!"

I continued, "When I go shopping with my friends and I see something I want that might be a little high in price, I call and ask if it would be okay with you if I buy whatever it is. Now, you don't see my girlfriends teasing me and asking me why I need your permission. See Craig, I choose to call you. You can't make me, and no matter what my girlfriends say, that's the choice I make.

"Understand one thing – I know you are the head of our household. I choose not to compete with you on that level, and I am comfortable with your leadership. I respect your decisions, and I have confidence that you have our family's best interests at heart; you've proved that to me over and over again. I love the way you take care of us, and I know how tough it must be sometimes for you to be responsible for our family. But you didn't even consider what I said as another way of looking at the situation. You never know, something I say may help you analyze a situation deeper from another perspective.

"Craig, you know that I am not a dumb woman, and sometimes I have some pretty good ideas. When we are discussing something, I want you to hear my point of view and consider that I have some say in your decision-making process. Remember, I want the best for our family, too. And after all the discussions, you still have the final word. I choose to follow your lead.

"Craig, I love you very much, but I will not allow you to wipe your feet on me. God made my brain and gave me the ability to think. You never know if He is sending you an idea or a solution to a problem through me."

Well, needless to say, we made up. That night, after making up some more, he said, "Thank you." I said, "You're welcome." He laughed and said, "No, well yeah. . . thank you for that, too. But thank you for standing up to me. Men can be very domineering – overpowering, sometimes, but no man wants his wife to be a doormat. Thanks for standing your ground." I said, "You're welcome." Then we made up some more. That time, I was the one to say, "Thank you!"

When we argue, I don't hit below the belt, meaning I don't insult his character. I would regret that later, and that would only cause him to have a wounded ego. A man with a wounded ego is not a pretty sight, and I would have to try to patch it up long after the argument was over. And another thing, a man with a wounded ego is more susceptible to the advances of other women.

Affairs

Do I think Craig has ever had an affair? I don't know. I would never sit here and say that I know for a fact that he hasn't, but I don't think he has. I'll tell it to you like this, I hope he hasn't, but if he has, whoever she is received the short end of the stick. Sure I would be hurt, but no more than he would be if I went out and did the same thing to him. No matter what comes, I don't think either of us would intentionally hurt the other. So that's the reference point we would have to start from – the point of "why?"

About a year after Craig started working for one of the major corporations, he invited me to come and have lunch with him. This is when I received outside evidence that my Simple Sacrifices really work.

I knew the people in his department by name and stories only because Craig told me about different situations throughout the year.

When I drove up for lunch, Craig was there to meet me at the car. Girl, I had on my two-piece, navy designer suit with my executive-style white blouse and navy pumps. My hair was just right, and my makeup was flawless. I knew it, too. I parked the car and stepped out as Craig opened the door. I wasn't out of the car good before he said, "Wow! You look like a million bucks!"

Craig took me into the building to the restaurant downstairs, and there they were – his co-workers. . . the women I had been hearing about all year. All of them were at one table, and they were beautiful women. Sharp dressers.

As we approached the table, I could see them whispering back and forth to one other. When we reached the table, Craig said, "Ladies, this is my beautiful wife, Abby." He introduced each of them by name. When he got around to the last person, she stood up and said, "You have a wonderful husband. I don't know how you do it, but if you ever write a book I'll be the first in line." I smiled and thanked her, but in my head I was saying, "It's women like you that keep me on my Ps and Qs!" Yeah, I know that was ugly. But, girl! You know she must have tried to make a few passes at Craig.

There was this one time when Craig took me to the wedding of his former marketing manager. The wedding was beautiful, but during the reception, one of his co-workers whom I had never met approached us. She said, "I hope you realize what a great guy you have here." When she left, Craig looked at me and said, "I told you she was crazy. Didn't I?"

I still don't understand why someone would want someone else's husband. I wouldn't want anybody's leftovers. Me, I want my own plate, and I don't want to know that someone else has been nibbling off of it either.

More and more men are using pagers as tools for managing their affairs. The "other woman" dials in a code so he will know what time to meet her. From there, all the man has to do is figure out what to tell his wife or girlfriend to get out of the house. But if you learn to think like the "other woman," you can beat her at her own game. And the Simple Sacrifices are your secret weapons against this destructive enemy.

Part 4

The Simple Sacrifices in Depth

> *The wise woman builds her house, but the foolish pulls it down with her own hands.*
>
> *Proverbs 14:1*

Now, listen. I'm going to ask you a few questions. I don't want you to take offense to what I ask, and I'm not inferring that everything is your fault. I know it takes two to make a good marriage, but it wouldn't do *you* any good to hear what *he* could do to improve your marriage.

Now, you can answer these questions to yourself as I go along. And since I'm not a marriage therapist, I'll just tell you how I address each of these questions in my own marriage. Here we go.

The Questions

Number one, do you show your husband how proud you are of him through your words and actions? Are you fun to be with? Do you make your life with your husband a wonderful adventure? Do you create an atmosphere of peace and quiet in your home? Do you continue to go out of your way to look attractive, just like you did before you were married? Do you accept him for himself, or do you try to make him over? Do you show him genuine appreciation for everything, whether big or small? And last, but definitely not least, question number eight: do you keep your sex life sizzling?

Our Differences

Did you notice that I said nothing about affection? Men don't give a hoot about affection. We do. We want to be loved, cherished and adored. Men want to be honored. They want to be admired and respected. And girlfriend, they want great sex!

Even the Bible tells us to reverence our husbands, and by the same token, tells husbands to love their wives. See? Right there in Ephesians 5:33, God is telling us the difference in man and woman. He made us, so He should know.

I didn't realize all of this during my first year of marriage. I was showering Craig with affection, which is what I thought would make him happy. After all, affection is what makes me happy. Now, he on the other hand would make a lot of sexual advances toward me, which frustrated me and made me feel used. He made the sexual advances because he thought that's what would make me happy. After all, that's what makes him happy. Through my reading, I came to realize that I was frustrating Craig just as much with my showers of affection as he was frustrating me with too many sexual advances.

Now, he understands that I want to be held, hugged and kissed without it always turning into lovemaking. Now, he knows I like to hold hands in public. I love feeling cherished and special. Once I communicated that to him, he understood the difference and knew what to do. But the most important thing I can say is, I made the necessary changes first, which made him want to please me. So, when I told him that I needed more affection, that's what he sought to shower me with – love, kisses, hugs, gifts and much, much more. He just needed to be told what I wanted in a non-judgmental way.

It's Up to You

I'm going to tell you how I have applied what I learned after our first year together. Develop the Simple Sacrifices to fit your own life and situation, and don't stop doing what you've learned. Girlfriend, he will not be able to resist you. In his eyes, other women will not be able to hold a candle to you. That's the way it should be in marriage. Marriage should be a beautiful, adventurous, life-giving union of two people honoring, loving, admiring and cherishing each other until death pulls them apart.

If you really want your marriage to work, you can make it happen. Now, don't get an attitude. Don't sound like my sister did years ago, "Why does the woman have to always be the one to do everything?" Like I explained to her early in her marriage, "You don't *have* to do anything. What you put into your marriage is what you get out. You put a lot in, you get a lot out. You put a little in, you get a little out. You put in hell, you get hell back. You put in heaven, you get heaven back. Whatever you put in, that's what you get back." So, like I told her, it's up to you. You make the decision about what you want. Fair enough? Okay.

I believe that when you start applying the principles behind the Simple Sacrifices, you will see a difference in your man, your marriage and yourself. When I finish with you, you'll be able to stand among hundreds of women, and your man will still pick you as the woman he would want to spend the rest of his life with.

Listen, as a woman, you have the God-given power to recreate paradise right here on earth for you and your husband. Yes, you can.

Number 1

Let's see. Where do I begin? I'll just start with the first question. Do you show him how proud you are of him through your words and actions? When I first started applying the Simple Sacrifices to my marriage, this was the most difficult principle of all. Openly showing admiration was not comfortable for me.

I had read how important admiration was for men. I guess I thought Craig should have known that I was proud of him. After all, I married him, didn't I? I thought that was good enough. But you know, a man could say the same thing. He could say, "Why should I have to show her love? She should know I love her. I married her, didn't I?"

I didn't want to sound phony by just saying things to make him feel good. The thought of trying to come up with what to say seemed so unnatural. Like I said, this was the hardest principle for me to activate. But you know what I finally realized? I realized that all I had to do was put into words what I was really feeling. I am proud of Craig. I am proud to be his wife. I am proud of the way he takes care of his responsibilities. I am proud of Craig in more ways than I had ever realized. More and more reasons came to me.

When I finally got up the nerve to put into practice what I had learned, I walked over to Craig and locked my arms around his waist. I looked at him and said, "Honey, I admire you so much." That's the moment my marriage took a turn in the right direction. That moment when my husband kissed me, I knew I had been holding back something that he needed desperately. He needed me to tell him how I felt.

Never again have I kept my admiration for my husband inside. I freely tell him how I feel as the feelings come. If I'm not with him, I may leave a message on his voice mail at the office or on our answering machine at home, or I might write him a quick note. Now, displaying admiration is second nature. When I see my husband doing something I like, I tell him. When I think of something that I like about him, I tell him. I show him that I admire him when he makes a suggestion about going somewhere or doing something and I follow his lead. My actions are telling him, "Yes, I like that idea. Let's do it." It also says, "I trust you. I like your leadership. You are capable."

When you show your admiration for your husband, he will do more of what you told him you admired him for. He wants your continued admiration. But I guess it's the same with us. If a man tells us something that he loves about us, we continue to try and please him because we want to hear that we are loved. And, we want to keep hearing it and *keep* hearing it. Now, most men don't understand that aspect of womanhood. But when they see how we respond to and need expressions of love, whether it be words or actions, they generally don't mind making the effort. Once you start openly admiring your husband, you will not run out of things to admire. He'll make sure of that. But, you have to keep your eyes and ears open. He is always sending out clues.

Now I realize what a crying shame it was and perhaps how hurtful it was to Craig when I would just walk right past him when he would stand in the mirror naked after drying off from taking a shower. Those were chances to show my admiration for his muscles, for his broad chest. You know what I mean? I tell you what, if another woman was trying to lure him away from me, she wouldn't have passed up one of those opportunities.

Somehow, it comes natural when the man is not your husband. It's like you instinctively know what to do, how to do it, when and where to do it – all in the name of convincing him that you are the one he wants. . . the one he needs. No matter if you're just dating or trying to steal him away from his wife, we women know what to do and say to please the object of our affection.

During the two years when Craig and I dated, I don't ever remember saying "no" to a date he had planned. I was always happy and willing to follow his lead. All he had to do was call me and ask. I was always ready.

All that changed during our first year of marriage. Then, Craig heard, "Oh, baby, I don't want to go there," and, "Why do you want to do that?" Then about six months into our marriage, I began complaining, "We never go anywhere anymore," and, "Why do I have to always be the one to suggest or pick where we go?"

Do you see what I'm getting at? When we were dating, my eagerness told Craig that I respected his decisions and that I didn't have a problem with following his lead. What he got after the "I do" was just the opposite, but of course I could not see that then. You do realize that was completely unfair of me to be one way while dating and another way upon marriage? On top of that, I had the nerve to fuss at him because he reacted to my change in behavior by changing himself.

As much as I loved him, I still don't know why I could not see that my actions were hurting him. He felt betrayed. The woman he carefully picked to spend the rest of his life with – the woman who once made him feel like a king – now acted as if he was nobody special. If I had realized what I was doing, things would have been different. There was no way I would have intentionally hurt him, but I just didn't understand. It's as if after the game of courting was won, I sat down and rested underneath the victory flag.

When Craig and I were dating, I was full of compliments. "I love the way you. . ." "You are really good at. . . " "I like it when you. . ." "You sure know a lot about. . ." "You did a great job on. . ." "You look great." "That just proves how terrific you are!" I could talk to him all night long. I appreciated the little things. I meant what I said, and the expression came naturally.

Why is it that I knew how to express my admiration before we were married, but a year later I needed to relearn to openly express my admiration? You know he had to be starving for my affection.

Admiration means the same as honor and respect. These are just as important to a man as being loved, cherished and adored are to a woman. It's miraculous how much expression of this can impact a man. A man never grows sick of admiration, just as a woman never grows tired of affection.

It takes extra effort to keep reminding Craig of my admiration. When I feel myself getting lazy, I do two things to snap myself back in shape. First, I remind myself of how I treated Craig when we were dating. Second, I ask myself what the "other woman" would do. What would she say to lure him?

Even in the middle of our arguments, I express my admiration for Craig. I might say, "I think highly of you, Craig, but what you just said really hurt my feelings," or "Craig, I look up to you so much, so it really hurts me when you. . ." My aim is to get my feeling across to Craig without wounding him in the process.

You would be surprised at how uttering words of admiration during an argument helps keep the focus on what you are really upset about. When you are hurling insults, the pain of the insults gets mixed up with the real reason for the disagreement. That makes matters worse, allowing the hurt to continue even when the disagreement has been settled. It's very hard for a man to resort to insulting his woman in the middle of an argument if she has expressed her respect for him.

What I really want you to understand is that I don't play games of lies and deceit with Craig. I *truly* admire him. The only game I play is with thinking up all the different ways to express how I feel for him. Do you realize that thinking of ways to please someone and make him feel good inside enriches your own life? What you give, you get back! I've found that the more I show my admiration, the more love Craig pours on me. This has reopened our line of true, deep and personal communication.

Long conversation with Craig was something I really missed, and I didn't even know it. I just thought it was a part of being married. Actually, to tell you the truth, I hadn't realized that we had stopped talking on a meaningful level because it happened so gradually, but I do remember wondering what was missing. I guess I was too busy running our household, planning our budget and handling our responsibilities. I wanted to stay on top of it all. I thought I was being the dutiful wife, but all the time I was actually leaving my man open to the trappings of another woman. He was vulnerable, and all she had to do was give him what he wasn't getting at home.

Can you imagine? There was probably some woman working alongside him every day, dishing out compliments and making him feel like a man. Meanwhile, I'm at home concentrating on whatever I thought was important at the time.

Expressing admiration has brought me the greatest joy in my marriage. When Craig and I talk, we have heart-to-heart conversations. You know how important good, satisfying conversation is to women. Now that Craig can feel my respect for him, he opens up more when we talk. He shares more of his feelings with me. He shares his dreams and desires with me, just like he did when we were dating. He does not fear me putting him down or making light of his thoughts and feelings. He knows I think highly of him, so he takes a chance on opening up to me. The more I respond by showing that I respect his feelings, the more he opens up.

The worst thing a woman can do is to make a man feel comfortable with sharing his deepest thoughts and feelings and then use something he said during an argument to hurt him. That right there can cause total shutdown to meaningful conversation – and even a meaningful relationship between a man and a woman. It's sad, but it happens all the time.

I love it when Craig opens up and tells me about his day. The time we share in one-on-one dialogue is important to me. The fact that he shares about his day says a lot to me. It tells me that he likes to unwind and relax with me and that he doesn't feel threatened or judged. When I compliment the way he handled a situation during the workday, it causes him to open up and trust me more. But if I feel he handled a situation wrongly at work, I don't lie to him. Instead, I just keep my opinion to myself. I just concentrate on listening and allowing him to get what he has to say off his chest. When I listen attentively, Craig returns the favor. He shows interest in my day.

There was one thing I realized after that first year – it's fun to have someone with whom I can share my feelings. When people we know see us in a restaurant or at a party, they always comment on how much Craig and I seem to have to talk about. When we visit my grandmother, it's the same thing. When my side of the family gathers for Thanksgiving, Craig and I enjoy sitting on the back porch talking. It never fails that after about 10 or 15 minutes, my grandmother hollers out the kitchen window, "Hey, you two! Come on in here. Y'all can do that at home." And we always reply, "Okay Mama, here we come." We end our conversation and go back in to join our family members, only to be teased; "Here come the love birds," and "Y'all must think you are still courting!"

Most wives don't realize that their husbands are starving for admiration. Well, now you know! And now you know what to do; fill him up. Don't tell me that he isn't admirable. Search hard; it's there. It may be that he doesn't complain when the house isn't neat, or that he irons his own shirts. You'll find something!

Number 2 and Number 3

Are you fun to be with? Do you make your life with your husband a wonderful adventure? This principle was not hard for me to understand, but putting it into practice took a little more effort. You see, my basic nature growing up was to be quiet and keep to myself. Let me explain. From the time I was a very small baby until I reached dating age, I suffered with bronchial asthma. Back then, if you were asthmatic you did not exert yourself for fear of having an attack and losing your breath. So early on, I learned to play games quietly by myself. As I grew older, I spent more and more of my time alone in my room. I mostly daydreamed, read magazines or primped in the mirror. I was very comfortable with me, and I enjoyed my own company. My sister called me boring and a square, but I did not care. I was content.

That carried over into my marriage. That first year, I played the role of the dutiful, no-nonsense wife. Boring, boring, boring! You know, I don't think I smiled – really smiled – at all that first year. I was too concerned with keeping things running smoothly. After all, I was an adult, and that brought with it a whole new set of responsibilities. I had to be serious. Boring, boring, boring!

For some reason, though, it wasn't like that during our two years of dating. I was a different person. For two years, I was like Cinderella at the ball. . . fun and enchanting. I laughed and smiled through every date. I knew I was a joy to be with, because that's what I intended to be. We had so much fun together. And then something happened within 24 hours of the preacher saying, "Now I pronounce you man and wife." That's when the Cinderella story ended and I turned back into the quiet, homebody me. Poor Craig! Craig must have been screaming inside, "Where is that woman I married? I want that one, not this one!"

When I realized what I had become, I started being fun to be with, and I started to enjoy my marriage much more. See? What you put in, you get back out. Put in fun, get fun back.

To start practicing this principle, I began by returning to the mindset I had when we were dating. I had to intend to be fun to be with – not for a certain time period or until a certain date, but for the rest of our married life. Don't get me wrong. I didn't turn into a bubbling bimbo. Instead, I wanted to ensure that if Craig and I were shipwrecked on a deserted island, he would be happy that it was with me that he got marooned.

I really do want our life together to be an adventure, filled with wonderful memories. Sometimes I fall short, but because of the effort, we have beautiful times together. My main goal is that whatever we are doing, I want it to be fun.

My outlook, and the way I react to life, rubs off on my kids. I want them to know how to enjoy life and be responsible adults in the process. I hope they have learned from me that if they want to really enjoy life and focus their energy on that, then nine times out of ten, they will succeed at reaching that goal.

It's just like our high school days and getting ready for a special party. Remember how much fun it was planning what you were going to wear? Remember the anticipation? Think about it. Did you leave home intending to have a good time or a bad time? That's why I say that it's up to you.

As our kids grew older and they were able to be at home alone for short periods of time, I was able to add new dimension to our adventures. When Craig arrived home after an extra rough day at work, I often suggested that we go somewhere and relax for a little while. With the kids at home, we usually ended up at one of the neighborhood restaurants and spent an hour talking over an appetizer.

It's not what you do; it's how you do it. Anybody can slip off from home for a while and go somewhere to sit and talk. What you talk about, your tone of voice and your mannerisms are what's important. Forget about the past due bills or bad report cards. Instead, treat those times like a special date. Keep the conversation pleasant.

By the time we got back home, Craig and I were both relaxed and ready to enjoy some time with the kids. We could all relax and do the things we each liked to do.

When the kids were much younger, we had what we called quiet time. From seven until eight o'clock, the kids would read, write or do whatever in their own rooms. Craig and I would spend this time just being together, whether we watched television, read the newspaper or a book, talked or whatever. It was a quiet, relaxing and pleasant time. That was "our time" for many years. Even when the kids were preteens and their Saturday schedules made us feel like a taxi service, we made the best of it. We enjoyed pleasant conversation and being in each other's company.

Remember when you were dating? You didn't care where you were going nor what you were going to do. You just wanted to be together because you had fun. You smiled a lot, which showed your date that you were enjoying his company.

Another advantage to being fun loving is that when you become upset about something, your husband knows it instantly. He can tell because the smile or pleasant look is not there. Wanting the fun to resume, he will want to know what's wrong. You don't have to walk around angry for weeks thinking he doesn't care. Even now, he probably does care, but he just doesn't know when you are really angry, because that's the way you look all the time. Men cannot read our minds; we have to send out messages that are loud and clear.

Sometimes being pleasant can be next to impossible. Back when I suffered severely from PMS, I reassured Craig that my demeanor wasn't his fault. I stuck to myself more and apologized a lot. I let him know what's going on, and he's always understanding. For me, I have seen firsthand how being fun to be with can enrich a person's life.

In my opinion, life is not like a box of chocolates – not ever knowing what you are going to get. I see myself as the confectioner – the maker of the chocolates. That first year of marriage, I tried my hand at making chocolates for Craig as a gift. They were not to his liking, but because they were a gift from someone he loved, he did not mention how bad they tasted. He did not want to hurt my feelings, and he even tried to eat them. Slowly, he stopped trying them at all. And one day he confided in me, "I don't like the chocolates you gave me." At the notice of disapproval, I went to candy-making school and learned all I could.

Through my years of experience, trial and error and regular solicited criticism, Craig now enjoys his boxes of candy. Since I am the confectioner, I know what I put into my chocolates. A few are filled with admiration, a few with fun, and so on. If I know the ingredients used to make my candies, then I know what I can expect back. I grant you that sometimes a piece of candy may not come out as expected, but experience is the teacher. The point is for me to continue to deliver the best chocolates, filled with a variety of the best ingredients I can give.

Listen, don't let the "other woman" out-do you in this area. Being fun to be with is actually as much of a benefit for you as it is for him. Laughter and light-heartedness are good for the physical body, and they are good for the soul. "A merry heart does good, like medicine." Proverbs 17:22. You know? This is your life, too. What you do for others, you should do for yourself, too.

I told you earlier about how I make Craig bubble baths with candles on all four corners of the tub? Well, I do the same thing for myself sometimes. I enjoy me. When I enjoy me, everyone benefits.

I remember one time when the kids were small, we made a fun-filled memory that will go down in our family history. It was the Smith Family Restaurant. It started while I was hanging around the house one Saturday, feeling like I needed a lift. I thought to myself, "If I'm feeling like I'm in a rut, I know Craig probably is too." I prayed for God to help me spread a little joy in my home, and I thanked God for His answer in advance. Then I went on about my business. Before I knew it, an idea was flooding through my mind.

I cooked a big dinner – pot roast with onions and carrots, fresh green beans with new potatoes, creamed corn and cornbread muffins. While dinner was cooking, I took three pieces of construction paper, folded them in half and made three menus. The front of the menus said, "Smith Family Restaurant." On the inside, I wrote "menu" at the top, and then I listed each item we were going to have for dinner. To the side of each item, I described the dish and included the price. "Delicious pot roast smothered in onions and carrots. $5." Fresh lemonade was under beverages and gelatin was listed for dessert.

When dinner was almost ready, I told the family that I was preparing a special dinner for them, so they needed to take a bath and put on something nice. I told them to get ready and added, "Whatever you do, don't come out until I call you." I looked at Craig and said, "Please, pretty please!" He agreed and then I was off to help Clayton pick out the suit he had almost outgrown.

While they were dressing, I set the dining room table with our best china and candles. Then I gave each one some play money and reminded them not to come out until I called. "What is this money for?" they asked. I said, "You'll see!"

I went back to the kitchen and put my apron on. Next, I put on one of Craig's classical albums to play soft, sophisticated music. I lit the candles and picked up a pencil, a small note pad and the three menus. After turning off all the lights, I invited them in.

I could hear the bedroom doors opening and their mumbles as they made their way down the hallway. As they came toward the dining room, they saw the big sign over the dining room door. "Right this way, please," I said as I ushered them into the dining room. You would not have believed your eyes; my son actually pulled the chair out for his sister. Don't tell me kids don't learn from watching their parents.

When they were all seated, I passed out the menus. I stood back to let them make their selections, and then I took their orders. I took up their menus and went to the kitchen to prepare their plates. I could hear Craig saying, "That's right, angel. Your napkin goes on your lap." Then he asked Clayton, "So, son, what did you do outside today?" As Clayton was finishing his answer, I was serving dinner. Craig and Chloé said, "Wow! This looks good!" Then Clayton said, "I didn't order green beans." I replied, "The chef said for you to eat all of your vegetables, because she made them especially for you." I stood back while they ate, and I brought lemonade and gelatin as needed. Craig tried to get me to sit down and eat, but I wanted to play my role until the end. It was so much fun!

When they finished eating, I gave them each a bill. After they paid their bill with their play money, Clayton asked Chloé, "Would you like to dance?" Chloé giggled and said, "I'd love to." Can you believe that? And Craig said, "I'd like to have this dance with the best waitress in the world." You know I obliged. I tell you, that turned out to be a magical evening. We made memories. . . precious memories.

Being fun to be with goes along with sharing quality time together. Be a good recreational partner. Learn to enjoy the things your husband enjoys, or at least be a pleasant participant. If he is sharing his love for a certain sport or activity with you, even if you don't enjoy the activity, enjoy his enthusiasm. Enjoy him! He'll be glad he's with you.

Number 4

Do you create an atmosphere of peace and quiet in your home? When I first read about this principle, I wanted to rebel, but I soon realized that this is one of the strategies of the "other woman." For one thing, she does not nag him. Men hate to be nagged. When they become husbands, they still hate to be nagged. Think about it. Did you nag when you were dating? Probably not. Somehow, nagging is learned by us shortly after saying "I do."

Many of my readings have warned against nagging. Yet I don't think I really understood what nagging meant, even though that's all I did that first year. I just thought I was making Craig aware of what was going on. "Honey, today is Thursday, so the trash man is coming tomorrow." A few hours later, "Baby, please don't forget the trash." Later that evening, "Craig, remember the trash."

For the life of me, I could not figure out why Craig's disposition would change. I was just trying to help him remember what he had to do. But I came to the realization that nagging is saying something more than once. . . continually, even. That is precisely what drives men crazy about their mothers and their wives (their mothers when they are teenagers and their wives as adults). Some men, after finally getting away from their mother's fierce tongues, cannot seem to bring themselves to jump back into the fire all in the name of the commitment "till death do us part."

I could never understand how nagging could do that much harm nor why men hated nagging so much. Since I'm not in a man's body experiencing his feelings, I just had to rely on the information I received from God's Word. The Living Bible says, "A rebellious son is a calamity to his father, and a nagging wife annoys like constant dripping (Proverbs 19:13)." I think that says it all.

I think I would have understood the harm I was doing earlier if someone had confronted me and said, "Stop acting like his mother. He's a man, not a boy. He doesn't need your help to figure things out." Let me tell you, when I finally came to a full understanding of how destructive nagging is, I cut it out. . . at least as much as I could. I see you smiling! Sometimes I find myself slipping back into those old patterns, but I am quick to turn myself around.

You know what's funny? In over 23 years, I haven't reminded Craig once to take out the trash. And guess what? I can count on one hand how many times he has missed trash day. Sure, we may remind each other of something or even make a suggestion, but we don't badger each other about getting things done. He respects my rights as an adult to do or not do what I want, and I have learned to show my respect of him in the same manner.

As I learned to stop nagging and keeping tabs on what Craig needed to do, I realized I had a big void in my life. I had spent so much time and energy being his personal reminder, I hadn't taken time to concentrate on me. In other words, "I had to get a life." Now that my mind was free from so many self-imposed responsibilities, I had more time to develop my own interests. And you know what? Craig has managed just fine without my constant reminders, and I feel more like his wife than his mother.

Not only does a man hate being nagged, he hates fussing and fighting. Proverbs 17:1 in The Living Bible says, "A dry crust eaten in peace is better than steak every day along with argument and strife." And the King James Version says, "Better is a dry morsel, and quietness therewith, than a house full of sacrifices with strife."

I work very hard not to let anger linger between Craig and me. We work through the emotional hurt until we both know that we are not holding harsh feelings for the other. Holding onto hurt and pain causes barriers between couples. Open communication handled respectfully is the only way to understand how your partner feels.

Also, I cannot stress how important it is to have a smooth-running household. When things around the home are in order, guess what your husband feels? He has confidence in you as being capable, and that earns his respect. When he sees that you have things under control, it frees his mind to take care of those things he needs to do. I know I've talked enough about being organized, keeping a daily planner and making lists, so I'm not going to bore you (or even nag you about it). Just remember, when you run an orderly household, it makes life easier for you and your family. It's a skill worth practicing.

Tying in with this, your home should be clean and tidy, or at least as much as possible. Can you imagine your husband slipping away to the "other woman's" home? Sure, we don't want to think about it, but I doubt he would find dishes in the sink, clothes and toys on the floor and the bed unmade. Don't you think it would be a place made ready for passion? Remember, this is a woman who is trying to convince your husband that his life would be better and more fulfilling with her. She is in direct competition with you for your husband, and sometimes men fall for this trap. If your husband comes home night after night to disarray and unpleasantness, he may find a haven of comfort with his escape to the "other woman."

I tell you what, though; it's more than a matter of order and cleanliness that lures husbands away. It's the whole package of preparedness that the "other woman" offers. Her house is clean and presentable, and she is fresh and sexy. He can sense that she has prepared for his arrival. He feels important, respected, honored and appreciated. Get the picture?

This is where a lot of wives miss the boat. We get so accustomed to being around our husbands, we take them for granted. And that's the first thing we wives say, "You take me for granted." But I think the reverse is true; we take our husbands for granted. Think about it. When he comes in from work, do you stop what you're doing to greet him? Does your husband feel more like an interruption than a day brightener?

More than likely, a husband comes home to a messy house only to be nagged all evening for not helping clean. I bet he didn't get this from you when you were dating. And I bet he wouldn't get it from the "other woman."

Listen, I have never been the "other woman." But I do know if I was the "other woman" just what I would do to try to lure Craig or any man from his wife. I believe it's instinct. At the same time, it's exactly what I didn't do during our first year of marriage.

If I were the "other woman," I would know what to do to get and keep his attention. I would even say that nine times out of ten, my tactics would work. For one thing, I would always show my interest in the conversation, whether we were on the telephone or in person. A few years back, there was a time when I answered the phone only to hear Clayton say, "Oh, that must be daddy." After I hung up the telephone, I asked how he knew it was his father. He explained, "Because you always talk like that when daddy is on the phone." I asked, "Like what?" He smiled as he said, "Low and sweet."

As the "other woman," I would also make sure that he is comfortable and relaxed in my presence. When I open the door to let him in, I would greet him with a warm sexy smile and a heartfelt kiss. I would also add an "I've missed you," just to confirm my actions. When we were dating and trying to "catch" our men, we gave them the best of ourselves. But after marriage, we give our best to others – people at work, our friends, our extended family. We give our men our leftovers, and we barely even offer them a smile.

How do you think your husband feels when you hang up the phone to announce that someone is on her way over and you run around the house for 10 to 15 minutes trying to make the place presentable? I'm sure he remembers a time when you went through the extra effort for him. Like I said, after marriage, we give our men our leftovers.

After I looked at my role as a wife from a different point of view, I made up my mind to give my husband the best me I have to offer. Remember the old saying, "What you did to get them, you have to do to keep them." That is exactly what I want to do – keep him. I am nowhere near perfect, but the effort does pay off.

Now that I know the Simple Sacrifices, I have a goal to continually work toward. I don't look at the Simple Sacrifices as something I have to do, but rather as something I choose to do. I choose to do the things that bring Craig joy in his home and with me. The wonderful thing about all this is that when I changed, Craig changed, too. When I returned to the attitudes I held while we were dating, Craig followed. We show mutual respect, admiration and love for one another. I do what I do for Craig because I know both the benefits and the consequences if I don't.

What I do for Craig, I do out of love. The Simple Sacrifices give me a better way to live my life with my soulmate and my friend for life. I want the best for my best friend, and he is certainly worth my efforts.

All the changes I have made since that first year have not only made me a better me, but they have definitely brought out the best in him. His co-workers and friends often comment, "Craig, you always seem so happy! What's your secret?" His secret is his relationship with God and his self-confidence in knowing that he is important to someone – to me, his children and himself.

As hard as it was, I learned a lot from our first year of marriage, and I'm thankful for that. You know, it's strange, but before Chloé was born, I bought books about being an effective parent. Yet I waited until after my marriage was in trouble to pick up a book on how to be a good mate.

Yes, we women want our men to be perfect. We want them to know what to say, how to say it, and when and where to say it. We want them to know what to do, when to do it and how to do it. We want their best. Why can't they expect the same from us?

I treat my family as royalty. Craig is the king, I am the queen and Chloé and Clayton are the princess and prince. Our home is our castle, and therefore is kept orderly and comfortable. The prince and the princess are groomed by the king and queen to one day become keepers of their own castle. They are taught mutual love and respect by example. That is how I rationalize our family structure.

I once thought everything should be 50/50 with two heads of the household. I've learned that two heads of the household cannot operate a happy home. Don't get me wrong, now. There is a difference between happy and functional. A purely functional home is a boring home. I know. I've been there. When I treat Craig like a king, he in turn treats me like a queen. I would rather be treated like a special queen than like a business partner. I did not like being an ordinary married couple. Ordinary is boring. Special is spectacular!

Of course, there are many other royal couples in the world. My best girlfriend shares a lot of the same views about marriage. They go out of their way to make each other happy. You can tell he is content – even happy – in his marriage. There is nothing in his power that he would not do for his wife. She is another blessed woman, and she knows it. Of course, she does her part too.

You would think they were still dating instead of being married. They are not pretentious people. Rather, they are just living a love affair. Anyone who is around them for more than a few minutes can see the love and respect they have for each other. Her man is the king of his castle, and he does not take his responsibility lightly. She is his queen, and he treats her like royalty. Another woman would not have a chance. He can't even notice another woman because he is too busy adoring and catering to his wife. The royal family has a new addition – their little prince (and my godson). I'm sure his life will be blessed from having such a wonderful example of love and respect.

Women just do not realize what a powerful role we have in the family structure. We are so busy trying to take the power from the man that we don't use the power we have to our full advantage. Women have the power to mold children into responsible adults, the power to encourage our men and the power to brighten our loved ones' day. Our children and our husbands can tackle the day better when they know they are important to and loved by us. I know that makes my day go better.

I'm not going to debate with you on this one. You have to remember I've been on both sides of the fence. Women who want to be equal with their husbands want a roommate, not a happy marriage. When I realized that my husband was unhappy and I was the lock that kept him there, I wanted to find the key. That key was to give my husband support at home by providing an atmosphere of peace and quiet.

Now, if your husband is an abuser or an alcoholic or someone like that, then I wouldn't know what to tell you to do; I wouldn't even try. But otherwise, if you have the desire, you can work your situation out. You have to remember, I've been applying these principles for over 23 years.

When I first started, I wasn't comfortable so I took things slow. But as I applied a few of the principles here and there and saw the positive results, my love for my husband compelled me to do more.

Number 5

And another thing, do you continue to go out of your way to look attractive. . . like you did before you were married?

I am ashamed to say it, but this is an area where I knew better, and I neglected it after we married.

As a teenager, I studied photos of pretty women in the magazines. I observed their makeup from eye shadow to eyeliner. Then, I would go to the drugstore to buy what makeup I thought I needed and return home to practice. I would practice for hours. When I reached driving age, my mother sometimes asked me to go to the store for her. It would take me two hours to dress and put on my makeup. Many days, my mother called out, "Abby, hurry up! I just need a loaf of bread."

In junior high and high school, my makeup, hair and clothes had to be perfect, and that was the way it was throughout my dating life. After the wedding day, I don't know if I figured that I could relax because I had caught my man or what. It wasn't something that happened overnight, but gradually, I stopped wearing my makeup every day, and I didn't pay close attention to how I dressed. Poor Craig!

Craig never complained about my appearance without makeup and in baggy sweaters. It's not like Oprah Winfrey was around to lead the way back then. I remember watching her show a couple of years ago when she had a panel of husbands and wives on. The husbands were trying to tell their wives that the fire was going out of their marriage. Why? Because the wives were not concerned with their appearance like they had been before marriage. An expert talked to the women about their appearance and attitude towards their marriage. She told the wives to make the extra effort to look good and keep the sizzle in their relationship with their husbands.

As each woman appeared after her makeover, the husbands' expressions seemed overjoyed by the transformation. At that moment, I thought, "I sure wish I had seen this show back then. If I had, it would have made me hold a mirror up to myself and realize I needed to change."

I know those women honestly had not realized just how bad things had become in their marriage. I know how they felt. It's like having blinders on. With everything else going on in a young marriage, it is easy to forget about *us*. We don't realize how important it is to continue to be the beauty that our men fell in love with – the beauty he wanted to hold for the rest of his life.

My heart went out to those women as they each started speaking with understanding. One of the women told the expert that she would start putting forth more effort in her appearance now that she had seen her husband's reaction. The other wives agreed.

My mother makes a point to never get into our business, but my appearance had started to concern her. My mother was the admissions officer at the local college Craig and I were attending. In between classes, we would meet up in my mother's office to do homework or to talk with my mom and her coworkers. One day out of the blue, my mother's secretary struck up a conversation about makeup. That's when my mother chimed in, "Abby can put on some makeup! She's the one that made my face up for all the big dances we went to when she was living at home." Her secretary said, "But Abby, I've never seen you in makeup. Why don't you wear it anymore?" The room got quiet as they waited for my answer. All I could say was, "I don't know." And that was the truth. I didn't know why I had stopped or even why it mattered. Mama's secretary replied, "Bring your makeup up here tomorrow so you can show me how to make my face up." I still hadn't caught on to what they were doing.

The next morning I got ready for school, taking the time to put on my makeup. I gathered my makeup to take it to school with me, looking forward to the task ahead.

Listen, when I walked into my mother's office, her secretary flipped! She said, "Abby, you are beautiful! You look like a totally different person." "See, I told you she is a pretty girl," my mama added. I tell you, they were really laying it on thick.

"Sweetheart, you are too pretty not to make yourself up," Mama's secretary said. "There are too many young ladies on this campus who would love to be in your shoes. I want to see you in your makeup more. Okay?"

With that in mind, I decided to start wearing my makeup everyday. I can't thank them enough for going through so much trouble to open my eyes to my appearance.

But let me say this, even though men want attractive wives, it takes more than an attractive and well-groomed wife to make a man happy. I believe that out of all the principles I've learned and practiced, this is the least important. Now, it *is* important, but it is not the highest on the list.

And take care of yourself for you! Care for your hair, skin and nails, and watch your weight. I take care of me more for myself than anyone else these days. I have found out that I feel better about myself when I do. Craig just happens to benefit, too. When I feel that I look good, I have more confidence. Real men love confident women.

I have to admit, I constantly battle my weight. I could easily give up and give in, but I would not feel good physically nor emotionally. Plus, I know that Craig likes to have curves to look at. I certainly had them when we were dating.

Men are literally fascinated by the shape of a woman's body. God knew what He was doing when He made curves. A nice shape is not the only thing that drives Craig crazy, but it does keep the engine running. I maintain a small waistline which Craig has trouble keeping his hands off of.

I remember right after losing 65 pounds, Craig brought me a beautiful black teddy home from one of his trips. When I tried it on I said, "Oh, honey! Thank you." He took one look at me and said, "No, thank you!"

Like I told you before, Craig never once said a thing about my weight, but he did seem to enjoy me being smaller. I think my weight gain had a lot to do with me subconsciously not wanting to be sexually attractive or attracted to anyone else. It was like a protective barrier to protect me from myself and to protect me from hurting Craig. I didn't have to worry about how to respond to the sexual advances of other men. I believe I was afraid of my own possible behavior.

After I lost the weight, Craig went through a time of doubting. I guess he wondered if I would leave him for someone else. I had to reassure him that I did not want to be with anyone but him. But what I realized more than anything was that if I wanted to get involved with another man, I would have whether I was fat or slim.

With my weight where it should be, I feel more sensual. When men try to make passes at me, instead of getting nervous, I just use it as a gauge that reminds me that I've still "got it."

Remember, it is important for you to take care of yourself. When you take care of yourself, you feel good about you and about who you are. You are too special to let yourself go. Don't do it for him; do it for you. You both will reap the benefits of an improved self-image and a sexy, appealing body.

Number 6

On to my next point: do you accept your man for who he is? It's more than just putting up with him. Or are you trying to change him?

This was one of my biggest problems during my first year of marriage, but I'm sure I'm not alone. I don't know why we women feel the need to make our husbands over, but many of us do. Was he not good enough in the beginning? Did we marry him just to have a project to work on? Now, if Craig had tried to change me, he would have had a rebellious young lady on his hands, and that's putting it mildly.

I guess when I tried to change Craig, it made me feel perfect; that is, until I heard Craig say he would change if that's what I really wanted. Was that what I really wanted? No, it was not, and I am glad he didn't change. I don't think I ever realized that I was trying to change him.

He did, though. He was constantly bombarded with questions. "Why did you. . .? Why would you. . .? Why didn't you. . .? Where are you going? Why? Why don't you. . .? Why do you have to do that? Why did you do it like that? Why are you doing that? Why can't you just. . .? Why don't you spend more time with me? Why did you put that there?" If I were in his shoes, I would feel like he was trying to change me, too.

I honestly had not realized that I was phrasing most of what I said to Craig in a critical way. I just thought of it as two people making conversation, you know? I asked a question and he answered it – conversation. But living with criticism is cruel and unusual punishment. And I've had to be careful of this with my children, too.

Once I realized what I had been doing with my words, it was not hard to change. I knew that I loved Craig for the man he was. That wasn't the problem. The problem was how I said what I said, and what I did not say. I guess that was another case of, "I know you know I accept you or why else would I have married you? So instead, I'll just tell you the things I don't like about you." How terrible!

I guess we spend so much time during the dating game telling them how much we admire them that we use marriage to play "catch up" on what we dislike. I tell you, no wonder so many men fear marriage. They have been trying for years to tell us that women change after marriage. They're right!

Just like I don't want Craig to find faults in me, I don't look for Craig's faults. Instead, I concentrate on his good qualities. The more I concentrate on the good, the more good I see. I like who he is more and more with each passing day.

When Craig wants to do something, I just accept that it is what he wants to do. For instance, Craig's career is such that I could scream bloody murder if I wanted to. He has to travel quite a bit, and he has to work long hours sometimes. And when on vacation, it's often hard for him to leave his work behind.

I remember a weekend when Craig and I flew to New Orleans for two days. The first morning we were there, Craig checked his messages as we were on our way to breakfast. Guess what? A problem had come up. He spent the entire day at a pay phone in the hotel lobby ironing out the problem. Meanwhile, I went in the gift shops and then came back to see if he was finished. I went to eat lunch and then came back to see if he was finished. I walked up and down the street and then came back to see if he was finished.

But, guess what? That man loves his job. And guess what else? I love that man. Each time I returned, I flashed him one of my "I love you" smiles. He smiled back and kept talking. That was my way of showing him that I understood. He kept saying, "Baby, I'm sorry. I'll make it up to you." When he finally hung up that phone at 5:30 p.m., we went out and enjoyed the rest of that evening, well into the night and early morning. We had a blast.

On the other hand, one thing Craig has had to accept about me is that I don't like saying goodbye at the airport. We've been married 23 years, and I still get teary-eyed when he has to leave. I would rather cry my good-byes at home than at the airport in front of all those people.

I still to this day get nitpicky and grumpy when Craig has a trip coming up. We have both come to accept the fact that I don't like being at home alone. Sometimes, I just get real quiet, trying to hide my agitation. Once he is gone, I'm fine because he calls me morning and night, and he leaves messages throughout the day. I just hate the good-byes and sleeping alone. Yet absence makes the heart grow fonder. It helps keep the romance in our marriage.

It's important that I not only have accepted Craig the way he is and have adapted to his ways, but I also show him my acceptance with my words and actions. Can you imagine going through a whole lifetime trying to be someone you are not in order to please someone else? That would be a shame. . . a crying shame. No one should expect anyone to do that!

Number 7

Next, do you show him genuine appreciation for everything, both big and small? When I first read about showing appreciation, I thought, "Piece of cake!" I was taught to say "thank you" at a very young age. Every time Craig did something for me, I always said, "Thank you!" or "I appreciate that."

You know what? I have since learned that showing appreciation stems from so much more. The gesture of just saying "Thank you," without the added oomph, is not enough. Have you ever been around someone who said things merely because it was the polite thing to do? It's as though it was a habit without any conscious reflection. That was me! I did not understand the art of true appreciation. Did you know that when you sincerely show appreciation for someone, it gives you a good feeling inside?

When I see Craig cutting the grass on Saturday mornings, knowing he could be a thousand other places doing a thousand other things with a thousand other women, I feel the genuine appreciation I express. Can you imagine how Craig must feel inside to know that I truly appreciate everything he does for our family and me? His response to that is incredible. I tell you, girl, it's wonderful!

The first step to truly appreciating others is to accept the fact that no one owes you anything – not your husband, your children, your parents, your siblings, your friends, your co-workers. . . not even your enemies. No one! See? When you truly internalize that fact, you will never again take the actions of another human being for granted. When someone is moved to do something for you, your sincere appreciation will shine forth.

To be appreciated; ah, it's a grand feeling! When I cook a dinner that Craig and the kids rave over, their appreciation always makes me feel that it was worth the trouble.

Being appreciated feels so good, but don't fall into the trap. Don't do anything for anyone just to elicit a response. I want to do what I do from the heart with no strings attached. When I do that, I am not disappointed by the outcome. Also, don't use appreciation as a source of manipulation. Appreciation must be genuine, sincere and from the heart.

When you want to express your love, it sometimes helps to have a plan B, and sometimes even a C and a D. Any time you deal with human beings, things are bound to turn out differently than you expected.

A friend and I were having lunch on Valentine's Day, and we discussed what we were going to do for our husbands that night. My friend said, "Abby, I'm going to fix that man the nicest bubble bath with candles and soft music." I said, "Oh, yeah? That sounds nice. I do that for Craig sometimes." She said, "Yeah, but I'm going to put him up a banner over the tub that says 'I love you.' You know, Abby, most women just wait for their husbands to bring them something for Valentine's Day. They just have their hands open waiting for a handout." I had to agree with her.

Then she asked me, "So, what are you planning to do for your Craig?" I said, "Well, actually, it's a little too X-rated to talk about, but I'll be wearing less than a string bikini. It's Valentine red, and it's hot!"

We giggled as we finished our lunch. The next day, same time, same place, I asked her how the evening went. She said, "Girl, it was a mess! Abby, I was so frustrated. Nothing went right."

"I needed to get Bill out of the house so I could get everything set up. I sent him to the grocery store to pick up some things for me. After he left for the store, I literally ran around the house getting everything ready. I made a path of red paper hearts from the front door leading to the tub full of bubbles," she explained. "But that man didn't come right back like I had asked him to. I waited and waited, and the bath water started cooling off. So I kept running the hot water periodically to keep it warm. Finally he came, but through the back door! Bill never comes through the back door," she said.

She went on to say, "Before I could turn around good and try and throw some of the hearts at the back door, the doorbell rang. Somebody was at the front door, and I scrambled to pick up the hearts. I called for Bill to help, and I threw the hearts at him saying, 'These were for you, anyway.' As if that wasn't bad enough, I opened the door, and there stood my son coming home from work. We laughed about it later, but nothing turned out right!"

I had to laugh with her. You know it's something special when you can laugh at yourself. Then she asked, "How about you? How was your Valentine's surprise?" I said, "All I can tell you is that it was terrific!" She said, "I'm glad somebody's plan worked out."

What she didn't know is that I had to resort to plan C. Plan A didn't work because Craig had eaten a heavy lunch and announced as he walked in the door, "I do not want anything else to eat for the rest of my life!" Well, I had to scratch the candlelight dinner for two in the bedroom. So much for that!

Moving right along to plan B, I pulled out my sexy little nothing, and guess what? The sales clerk had put the wrong size in the box – extra small. Listen, I can't wear a small, let alone an extra small. Well, I thought, "I'll just have to exchange it, and he'll get this hot little number another night."

On to plan C. I gave him a handmade card that said, "Thanks for making me your Valentine 365 days of the year." I did a little Valentine dance in our bedroom. I tell you, I put on a show. I put on my bikini swimsuit and drew hearts all over my body with a black washable marker. All I wanted was for Craig to know that he was special to me. He got the message loud and clear.

As I was doing my sizzling strip tease show for Craig, I told him the rules – no touching the merchandise for 24 hours. Boy, did that raise the level of excitement! He was fit to be tied. Every time his hands made a move toward me, I pushed them away. I tell you, I could hardly dance for trying to make him keep his hands to himself.

Listen to me, I know what it feels like to be uncomfortable after a large meal, and I didn't want Craig to feel obligated to have sex. I wanted to be sure he enjoyed the evening with no pressure. So, I added the rule to the game.

When I woke up the next morning, the first thing I had to do was push his hand off me. I said, "I told you, Mister! No touching until tonight." I did everything I could think of to drive him crazy, including doing my morning exercises in the nude. You should have heard some of the phone messages he left for me that day.

But let me tell you how it all turned out. That evening on my way home from school, I exchanged my Valentine's outfit for the right size. Once home, I warmed up the dinner I had prepared the day before, and we had dinner as a family. After dinner, the kids disappeared. I took the bottle of wine and two glasses to the bedroom. I locked the door and refused to let Craig in until I was ready. I took a quick shower and put on my robe. Then while Craig was taking his shower, I lit the candles, poured the wine and turned down the bed. As I passed the shower door to hang my robe up, I thought, "Why not?" I opened that shower door and walked right on in – outfit and all. What a night! I struggle to find a word. Spectacular! Yes, that's the word.

Just think about what I would have missed if I had given up when plan A failed. Instead, we both have two unforgettable memories.

The point I'm trying to make is to be flexible. If plan A doesn't work out, move on to plan B. It's the thought that counts. If the thought is for him to know that you appreciate him, follow through until the end.

When you get frustrated over a plan that didn't work, that means you were looking for a specific reaction. That's manipulation. Don't do anything for a reaction. Do it out of love. If you do it out of love, plan B, C or even D will come automatically because it will come from the heart.

Just remember to let your love shine through. Let your love show in your deeds. Let your actions be an extension of your love, and that part of your life will enrich you and love you back. Remember, you are responsible for your own happiness, and what you give, you get. We really do have a choice.

Yes, life is about choices. A lady in my church shared that she had always wondered about the Garden of Eden and why God allowed things to turn out as they did. God knew Adam and Eve were going to sin even before it happened. So why would He let sin come into the world if He could have prevented it from happening? She shared that after several years of wondering, she came to the conclusion that God had to set up a system that would give us a choice – the choice to do His will or to do our own will. If we make the choice to do His will, then He knows we are truly His. So I say to you, you have choices. Which way do you choose? The road to enter happiness, which is giving of yourself, or the road to an unfulfilled life?

Number 8

The last question is the most important one in a man's book. Do you keep your sex life sizzling? Do you make passionate love, or do you just have sex?

When we had only been married one year, our sex life was still exciting. Yet I learned what to do to keep the fire in my marriage over the years. You know how important affection is for most women? Well, sex is more important than that to most men. They need it to be happy. Sometimes it is hard for wives to remember how important sex is to their husbands. But I bet it is equally confusing for our husbands to try and figure out our deep need for affection.

Men want affection, but not to the degree that most women need it to be happy. By the same token, women want sexual fulfillment, but most of us don't need it to the degree that most men do. This is one of the areas where mutual understanding plays a big part in having a happy marriage.

God advised us in the Bible to be available sexually for each other. He knows the nature of men. After all, He made them. All I can tell you is that it is very important to keep boredom out of your bedroom. Most men cannot tolerate sexual boredom.

The books I read helped me keep a fresh mind and attitude about our sex life. Whenever I've felt like we were in a sexual rut, I read a new book to spark my imagination. The way I figure it, if I get anywhere close to being bored, I *know* Craig is. So when I can't seem to come up with new ideas, I read.

It's your attitude about your own sexuality and your body that makes the difference. If you don't feel sexually attractive, it's hard for your husband to see you as desirable. You have to come to terms with who you are sexually. You have to appreciate your body, improving the things you can and accepting the things you can't change.

A woman who shows confidence in herself is sexually appealing to men. Check your own attitude, your outlook, your mind set. When I feel like I'm losing the essence of my womanhood, I remember myself in my single days – the kind of clothes I wore, the way I watched my weight, the confidence I had in my appearance. I knew I had something that the opposite sex wanted. And I think that's what we lose after marriage. We lose our confidence in our natural appeal and the ability to meet our man's basic need, including his need for sexual gratification.

When we as married women get back in touch with our womanhood, we will remember the power of our magnetism. Then, we have a powerful tool in making our marriages affair-proof. The power is in our hands. We have the power to keep our men focused and attracted to us. If I could help you understand the depth of a man's natural need for sexual excitement and satisfaction, you would understand that you play a very important role in providing him with a source of constant pleasure for the rest of his life until death do you part. If you are being a constant source of pleasure, what do you get in return? That's right! You get pleasure. You can't beat that!

Your husband should never feel like he has to beg for sex, nor should he feel like his wife has lost her attraction to him. If you go through a dry spell, make sure you talk about what's going on. Don't make him try to read your mind. Don't let anything negative linger in your bedroom. Talk it out. Work it out. Get it out. Love it out. Wives have to combat the "other woman" by making sure her husband understands that he is not responsible for any sexual lows. Make sure he knows that you still find him sexually attractive and that you find value in your sexual relationship.

Understand how sex benefits you. It relieves the stress of the day. It's great exercise. It keeps you connected to your soulmate in a physical way. It strengthens the bond of your friendship. It causes the rhythm of your hearts to beat as one. It's relaxing. It's satisfying. It feels good.

What men and women both fail to realize is that most women don't have to reach climax every time they make love to be sexually satisfied. This is also where communication comes in. Let your husband know when you don't plan to reach an orgasm. Let him know that you enjoy his touch, and sometimes that's enough for you. In other words, don't make him feel like a failure. If you open up and talk about how you feel as a sexual partner, he will not just assume that you are just going through the motions. And if you understand your sexual self, you will understand that you don't have to just go through the motions because his touch and the physical closeness are very satisfying to the feminine body.

I strive to bring fun, excitement, variety and pleasure to our sexual relationship. It's an adventure – an adventure of two people living their lives on earth together, two people sharing and giving of themselves and loving each other. No, I don't look at marriage as a challenge in every sense of the word. Marriage to me is two people living and comfortably expressing their best with each other.

Giving your best in the bedroom is the spice of life. Listen to this. I remember one Halloween when the kids were small. I put the kids to bed at about nine o'clock. I asked Craig to go to the grocery store for diapers and a few other things. While he was gone, I took a quick shower and moisturized from head to toe, sprayed on a little perfume and touched up my hair and makeup. I lit two candles and place them on the nightstands on each side of the bed. Time was passing fast. I put on my black boots and my black trench coat. That's all! When I heard Craig drive up, I turned off all the lights in the house. I ran out the back door and slipped around to the front. I waited a few minutes, giving him a chance to notice I was gone, before ringing the doorbell.

"Who is it?"

"Me!"

"Who?"

"It's me! Open up."

As he opened the door, I opened my trench coat with both hands and said, "Trick or treat!" Girlfriend, if you could have seen the look on his face. It was so funny. He said, "Girl! What in the world?" He took my hand and led me back to those two candles. That's what I call creating memories. The "other woman" is not the only one with an imagination.

Oh, and listen to this one. One Saturday evening as I was dressing for a party, I remembered something I had read. I decided to give it a try. Craig and I arrived at the party about eight, and he rang the doorbell.

Right before the hostess got to the door, I said, "Oh, my goodness!"

"What?"

"I forgot to put on my panties!"

Before he could respond, the hostess was greeting us. Let me tell you, Craig followed me the whole night. I couldn't have gotten rid of him if I wanted to. And if there were any other women there wanting to get Craig's attention, too bad! He wasn't interested.

It's a wonderful adventure, whether I'm cleaning the house in the nude, serving him dinner with an apron as my uniform or creating a nightclub scene with strip show and all. Craig doesn't have to leave the house to find variety, excitement, fun and pleasure. Neither do I.

Understanding

Start doing the Simple Sacrifices and see positive changes in your relationship. You can help your husband understand more about your nature – the nature of womanhood.

Take conversation, for instance. By nature, men and women communicate differently. Have you noticed that we acknowledge that we are listening after each sentence or so? Men don't usually do that. One day, Craig and I were conversing. I kept talking, but Craig wasn't saying anything. Finally, I said, "You're not paying any attention to me." He said, "Yes, I am! I heard every word you said." Then he repeated almost word for word everything I said. I said, "Well, you must not agree with what I was saying then." He replied, "No, that's not true. I agree 100 percent."

I knew I was losing this battle, because I couldn't figure out how to help him understand how I was feeling without nagging or being critical. So I said, "Okay, honey. I'm sorry."

A few minutes later, he started talking about how he wanted the backyard landscaped. He talked and talked and I listened, not making one sound. Finally, he said, "Abby, are you all right?"

"Yeah, I was just listening to you."

"Oh, okay." He continued talking before finally saying, "Baby, what's wrong?"

"What do you mean?"

"It seems like you're ignoring me. Did I say something wrong?"

"No, you didn't say anything wrong. I just need for you to understand how I feel when you don't respond to me as I'm talking. It makes me feel like I'm in a one-way conversation. When you don't respond, I don't know if you agree with what I'm saying or not. It makes me feel real uneasy."

"Point well taken. I'm sorry."

Conclusion

You know, I used to wonder why I experienced some of the things I have in my life. At times, I wondered why my desire to have more than the average, mediocre marriage was so strong – a drive that keeps me reading into the wee hours of the morning, searching for answers. I wondered why everything I did seemed to be an experiment, keeping the good and weeding out the bad. I wondered why He blessed me with a yielding heart – a heart that stops at the drop of a hat and says, "Yes, Lord." These were questions that embraced me, knowing in my spirit that the answers would one day come.

My answer did come. It's all happened so that I may be of service to others. It is my desire for more women to have happy, fun-filled marriages. I want women to know and use the Simple Sacrifices as a way of life. I want more wives to realize the power they have to create happy homes and use that power to create heaven on earth. I desire it for you. I see it. I feel it. I believe it.

Are you ready to face the challenge?

Affirming Simple Sacrifice #1

How will I show my man that I love him for who he is? What will I say? What will I do?

I will ____
I am grateful for accepting my soulmate.

Affirming Simple Sacrifice #2

How will I show my man how proud I am of him through my words and my actions?

I will ____
I am grateful for new beginnings.

Affirming Simple Sacrifice #3

How will I show my man just how much I appreciate him? What will I say? What are some things I will do?

I will ____
I am grateful for the joy that love keeps bringing.

Affirming Simple Sacrifice #4

What can I do to make myself more fun to be around? What will I do to make our lives more fun and adventurous?

I will______________________________________

I am grateful for the simple pleasures of life.

Affirming Simple Sacrifice #5

How will I share myself with my man? With my family? How will I let them know who I am?

I will______________________________________

I am grateful for remembering who I am.

Affirming Simple Sacrifice #6

What will I do to create an atmosphere of peace and quiet in my home? What changes will I make?

I will______________________________________

I am grateful for harmony being restored in my home and in my life.

Affirming Simple Sacrifice #7

Have I been paying attention to my appearance? What will I do to make myself more attractive?

I will ______________________________________

I am grateful for my new awareness.

Affirming Simple Sacrifice #8

What are some of the things I will say and do to keep the "sizzle" in my sex life?

I will ______________________________________

I am grateful for an intimately fulfilling sex life.

Appendix

Abby's Between Girlfriends

Premarital Questionnaire

You and your fiancé should use this questionnaire before marriage to help measure your readiness for this lifelong commitment. Be honest yet loving in your replies. Each of you should write your answers on a separate sheet. When you are finished, exchange answers and discuss them. Respect each other's right to express personal feelings and opinions regardless of whether your response is similar or not. Talk through issues to find out if you are ready for marriage to each other.

1. What is my idea of a good marriage?

2. What do I think will change after I am married?

3. What do I hope will never change about our relationship?

4. What am I willing to do to have a happy marriage?

5. What am I not willing to do in marriage?

6. What type of spouse would I like to have?

7. I hope my spouse and I will ________________.

Annual Marriage Update

Use this questionnaire at least once a year to help measure the sturdiness of your marriage. Remember to be honest yet loving in your replies. Each of you should write your answers on a separate sheet. After all the questions have been answered, exchange answer sheets. Each of you go to a quiet place and review the questions and answers given. After you have both had time to consider each other's responses to the questions, come back together and discuss your findings. Remember to respect each other and not to point fingers of blame. Work together to build a more compatible and loving union.

1. Have I enjoyed my marriage this year?

2. What do I like most about my marriage?

3. What do I like least about my marriage?

4. What would I like to see change for the upcoming year?

5. What am I willing to do to make my marriage better?

6. *What would I like to see my spouse do to make our marriage better?*

7. *This year I want my spouse and me to ______________________.*

Let's Keep In Touch

Ladies, I have enjoyed talking with you so much, it's hard to say goodbye.

I am in the process of writing "Abby's Girl Talk: A Sharing of Marital Secrets to Spark the Imagination/ Keeping The Fires of Love Burning Bright." Let's share ideas. After all, what are girlfriends for?

There are times when we all struggle for new ideas to spice up our marriage. We as wise wives need a steady stream of ideas to keep our imaginative juices flowing. This is where "Secrets to Spark the Imagination/Keeping the Fires of Love Burning Bright" comes into play. We will be helping women with ideas for themselves and their marriage, as well as creating wonderful memories that last a lifetime. If you have something to share, let's talk. How do you keep the fires burning bright in your marriage?

Please send all entries by mail or E-mail. Include your name and telephone number so I may contact you if needed. Write me at:

Coach Abby, Inc.
P.O. Box 1475
DeSoto, TX 75123

abby@abbygailsmith.com

For fun and to order products from Abby's On-Line Sensual Shop, visit my Web site at www.abbygailsmith.com. A site just for women. . . built with you in mind.

I'll talk to you soon,

Abby

To contact Abby Gail Smith about speaking engagements, keynotes, seminars and retreats, please call 425.962.2821 PRESS 1; E-mail abby@abbygailsmith.com or write to: Coach Abby, Inc.; P.O. Box 1475; DeSoto, TX 75123.

Recommended Readings for Abby's Girlfriends

Holy Bible

Total Woman
by Marabel Morgan

Can This Marriage Be Saved?
by the Editors of Ladies Home Journal
with Margery D. Rosen

Weight, Sex, and Marriage
by Richard B. Stuart

Fascinating Womanhood
by Helen B. Andelin

Back To Eden
by Jethro Kloss

The Magic of Thinking Big
by David J. Schwartz, Ph.D.

Secret of the Ages
by Robert Collier

7 Habits of Highly Effective People
by Stephen R. Covey

About the Author

Abby Gail Smith is the president of Coach Abby, Inc., a training and consulting firm. She teaches "Deep Meditation for Christians" classes and lectures in the area of creating happy marriages and happy homes.

Abby is a Corporate Sponsor and has been on the Board of Advisors for the Celebrating Life Foundation, promoting breast cancer awareness and funding for research. She continues to write and speak on marriage and strives to follow a holistic lifestyle.

Abby is a native of Texas, where she lives with her husband of 23 years. They have a daughter and a son who are college students on the East Coast.

A portion of the proceeds from the sale of this book will go to the Celebrating Life Foundation (visit their Web site at www.celebratinglife.org) and to the Hope Cottage Pregnancy and Adoption Center (visit their Web site at www.hopecottage.org).

Remember: For fun and to order products from Abby's On-Line Sensual Shop, visit my Web site at www.abbygailsmith.com. A site just for women. . . built with you in mind. Enjoy!

Notes